## "Would you stop encouraging him?"

Addie leaned closer.

"What?" Evan whispered back. "What am I doing? I'm just sitting here. I can't help it if the little guy likes me more than you."

He'd meant to be teasing, but based on the angry heat billowing in his direction, Addie hadn't taken it that way. She was definitely about to blow.

"Mommy, I don't be here." Sawyer's voice had dropped from the level ten he'd been operating at, but it was still enough to cause laughter from the people sitting closest.

Pink rushed Addie's cheeks, and sympathy flooded Evan. In an attempt to defuse, Evan opened his arms to Sawyer, who came right to him. The tyke was good for his ego. He tugged the stubborn guy up on his lap, and Sawyer sank back against Evan's chest like he was a safe place.

His heart gave a heavy thump that sounded oddly like a warning alarm.

While he might have plenty of reasons and determination not to fall for Addie all over again, Evan was way too close to the edge of that cliff when it came to her kid.

**Jill Lynn** pens stories filled with humor, faith and happily-ever-afters. She's an ACFW Carol Award–winning author and has a bachelor's degree in communications from Bethel University. An avid fan of thrift stores, summer and coffee, she lives in Colorado with her husband and two children, who make her laugh on a daily basis. Connect with her at jill-lynn.com.

## Books by Jill Lynn

### Love Inspired

#### Colorado Grooms

*The Rancher's Surprise Daughter*
*The Rancher's Unexpected Baby*
*The Bull Rider's Secret*
*Her Hidden Hope*

*Falling for Texas*
*Her Texas Family*
*Her Texas Cowboy*

Visit the Author Profile page at Harlequin.com.

# Her Hidden Hope

## Jill Lynn

LOVE INSPIRED
INSPIRATIONAL ROMANCE

# LOVE INSPIRED®
## INSPIRATIONAL ROMANCE

Recycling programs
for this product may
not exist in your area.

ISBN-13: 978-1-335-55362-1

Her Hidden Hope

Copyright © 2020 by Jill Buteyn

This edition published by arrangement with Harlequin Books S.A.

For questions and comments about the quality of this book,
please contact us at CustomerService@Harlequin.com.

Love Inspired
22 Adelaide St. West, 40th Floor
Toronto, Ontario M5H 4E3, Canada
www.Harlequin.com

**Printed in U.S.A.**

Behold, what manner of love the Father
hath bestowed upon us,
that we should be called the sons of God.
—*1 John* 3:1

To my girlfriends—thank you for keeping me sane and always supporting me. I don't deserve you all, but I'm definitely keeping you. Kelley— thank you for being my early reader and for making every book better. I absolutely couldn't do this without you!

And to my agent, Rachelle, and my editor, Shana—thank you for making my dream of writing books come true.

# *Chapter One*

Evan Hawke no longer considered a particular place home, but the city of Westbend, Colorado—where he'd spent his childhood—was fighting him on that idea like a boxer with a mean left hook. Everything about the frozen-in-time Main Street and the mighty silhouette of the Rocky Mountains lining the west shouted *Familiar, known, welcome back*. Everything inside him shouted *Don't get too attached*.

He stepped inside Herbert's Hardware store, momentarily forgetting his golden retriever Belay was attached like a bur to his left pant leg—the one that hid the prosthesis below his knee and allowed him to go through life with a semblance of normalcy.

No doubt Herb preferred no animals inside, and since Belay wasn't a full-on guide dog, she didn't count. Some stores didn't care either way, but Evan didn't like to push or draw attention. He could walk fine without Belay, had been doing so for years. But he hadn't known how much he needed the girl until she'd bounded into his world unapologetically after failing her guide-dog training.

"Come on, Bel." The day was in the mid-fifties and the sun was out. Even with yesterday's dump of late spring snow, Belay would be fine waiting for him outside. Evan never had to worry about her bothering anyone. The opposite was more often true—people didn't leave Belay alone. She was too much sunshine wrapped up in one animal—too hard for passing kids and adults to ignore.

Back outside, he found a dry patch for her under the awning. The snow was already turning to rivers, rushing like rapids down the street, splashing under car tires. "Lay." Belay obeyed but kept her head off the ground, perked, waiting to see if he'd change his mind. He tied her leash to the bike rack, just in case. "I'll be back in a minute. You'll be all right."

Her nose drooped as if she were a beauty queen he'd kicked out of a contest.

Back inside, warmth caused him to unbutton his lined flannel. Evan snagged a cart and scooted through the aisles until he found the tile he'd be installing at his mom's house. Herbert's didn't have an array of colors or shapes or sizes, but Evan was a simple man, and he'd begun fixing up his mom's place accordingly. He and his brother Jace had agreed to the plan before he'd started patching what could be patched and repairing what needed to be repaired. As long as it was livable and clean and sellable, they'd be good to go.

He was far more of an outdoorsman than indoor, but his mom's house had been sitting for three months after her death, and he and Jace had decided it was time. Time to renovate. Time to sell. Time to bury another part of their mother.

Deep, dark aching sadness like he'd only experienced once before to that level filled his throat, and the tiles swirled and changed shapes in front of him. He'd made it back to see his mom twice before she passed. At the end, when the doctor had told Evan to get home, that she was failing quickly, he'd done exactly that, but it had been too late to say goodbye.

It was hard not to regret that now. Hard not to regret a lot of things.

Jace was busy training to be an EMT. It had taken his brother some time to figure out what he wanted to do after retiring from bull riding, and Evan was just glad he'd picked another low-key profession. Insert eye roll. Not that he could blame his brother for needing the tick-tick of a kicked-up heart rate or the surge of adrenaline.

They both experienced that same tug.

Which explained why Evan climbed mountains and led groups of trauma victims past the edge of reason and into uncharted waters. There was something healing about doing what you couldn't or shouldn't do.

What didn't make sense to anyone else.

His mom, somehow, had understood that. Another reason he missed her.

Jace and his wife, Mackenzie, had already done enough getting rid of things and purging, cleaning out Mom's place. It was Evan's turn to step up.

He hefted the boxes he needed into his cart, then added a container of grout and some spacers. Footsteps pitter-pattered down his aisle, and a little boy—toddler aged—stopped next to him.

"Hi." He shoved the roll of blue painting tape in his hand up to Evan like he was offering a gift to a king.

"Hi." Evan smiled. The kid had chocolate hair that sloped across his forehead and matching eyes filled with curiosity. His golden russet skin made Evan's barely-able-to-hold-a-tan ruddy complexion pale in comparison.

"Thanks, but you keep the tape." Evan raised

a palm to encourage the boy to hold on to his find, but the kid thrust the item at him again. Not sure what to do, he flipped his hand over. The boy dropped the tape into his palm and then scooted a few steps down the aisle. Removing a mixing paddle from its hook, he trotted back to Evan and placed that in his hand too. Before he could protest, the boy quickly added knee pads and a foam sponge to his loot.

Did this kid have a mom or dad nearby? A scan of the aisle didn't reveal anyone. Should he go up front and tell the person behind the counter? If someone wasn't looking for the boy now, they surely would be any minute.

While the tyke occupied himself by destroying any organization on the shelf near his level, Evan stealthily set down the items he'd been gifted and continued filling his cart with the supplies he needed. He wouldn't leave the store without saying anything, but at the same time, he had work to get back to.

When the little boy took a step into the main, larger aisle along the back of the store, a woman called out. "Sawyer! There you are. Remember you can't leave Mommy. You have to stay right by me in the store." There was something so familiar about the woman's voice…or maybe Evan just recognized that concerned mom/stressed wobble he'd heard her stifle. But she had managed to keep herself calm and not rage at the kid for disappearing. Evan respected that. His mom had been calm too. She'd had a lot to deal with, especially with Dad, but she'd always been good to her sons.

Dad, on the other hand, had been pretty worthless before getting himself killed in a bar brawl. Perhaps that was one of the reasons it wasn't easy for Evan to come home. Jaded memories like that didn't leave a kid when you asked nicely and said please. They stuck around for the long haul. Made it hard to remember that he and Jace had made something of themselves that their dad didn't deserve one ounce of credit for.

The boy, sensing he was about to be caught, made a break for it down the aisle Evan still occupied. Should he get out of the way? Block?

Instinct had him slowly easing his cart so that it fit the whole space. The toddler had to pause to devise a new escape plan, and it gave his mom enough time to catch up to him. She swung him up into her arms.

"Sawyer, you *have* to stay by Mommy." Her eyes flashed to Evan's. "Thanks for the assist." Shock registered in her slacked jaw, and all five foot three inches of her froze. A whole truckload of Evan's past rammed into him in the form of the lithe woman with waterfall black hair and honey-brown skin, compliments of her Filipino American heritage.

"Addie." Her name croaked out of him.

"I didn't know you were in town."

They said the exact same thing at the exact same time.

"Hi." The boy—Sawyer—obviously hadn't had any lessons about uncomfortable situations, because he squirmed to be let down while greeting Evan once again. Or maybe the little tyke knew just what he was doing cracking the ice that had quickly formed.

"Hi." Evan's response seemed to placate him, because he lifted his hand to wave, then studied his own little fingers.

She put him down on the ground, and he snatched up the blue tape, holding it in Addie's direction. "I want tape, Mommy. Bue tape."

"You can get your bue tape, but I need you to stay in this aisle for me, okay?"

"Okay, Mommy." Sawyer began stacking and knocking over the items he'd previously removed from the bins and hooks.

"So you're…visiting?" Addie's question was burdened with so much more than the innocent words, and Evan didn't blame her. The same curiosity pressed down on him.

"Yeah. I live in Chattanooga, Tennessee." Though most of the time his apartment was empty while he traveled and led groups across the U.S. "I'm back because my mom died." That probably wasn't the best way to make that kind of announcement, but his brain was nowhere near working condition right now. Addie had always had that effect on him. He'd been hooked on her from the first time they'd met after the rodeo one night. He'd been dating Maisy Tilly at the time, but after one conversation with Addie, he'd broken up with Maisy.

He still didn't think Maisy had forgiven him for that.

"I heard that. I'm so sorry, Evan."

"Thanks. I miss her." Again with the randomness coming from his mouth. Evan wasn't usually the most sensitive or emotional of creatures, but walking smack into his past messed with his vocal cords. And his ability to think, process or move, it seemed, because he was still glued to the same position he'd been in when they'd recognized each other. He peeled his hand from the cart and dropped it to his side, begging the limb to act as if it knew how to function in social situations. "I'm getting her house ready to sell. Jace and Mackenzie—my brother and his wife—did a bunch of the purging work already. And now I'm just here for the final touches." How many things could Evan spit out that Addie didn't care to know about him? "What about you?" He managed to stem the onslaught of useless info by changing the direction of the conversation.

"I live here now." Why did that shock him so much? It almost…hurt. What a strange reaction. "I'm reopening the bed-and-breakfast."

During the summers in high school, Addie had lived at Little Red Hen Bed & Breakfast with her mom's cousin Alice and her husband, Benji, whom she affectionately referred to as Tita and Tito.

But after that last summer, when she'd met Evan and things had gone so incredibly wrong so fast… Evan wasn't sure she'd ever return.

"Benji and Alice were always good to you."

Moisture pooled in those eyes that were a bottomless, dark well of things that had been and were no more. They pulled him in and latched on tight.

"They were. That's why I'm reopening the place. Because it's what they wanted and what I wanted, and I just had to…" She shrugged. "I had to make that happen."

"Is that what your supplies are for?" She'd left her cart at the end of the aisle when she'd stopped to capture Sawyer, but it was filled with home-improvement supplies.

Sawyer handed Addie a random assortment of his finds, and she absentmindedly accepted.

"Yeah. Tita and Tito sold the B & B about two years ago. Tito had already been sick for a while at that point, and after he passed, Tita didn't last long. It was as if her heart didn't have a reason to keep pumping without him. The new owners started fixing up the bed-and-breakfast, but they didn't get far before running out of money and defaulting on the loan. So I'm finishing the projects they started and trying to freshen things up before I hopefully reopen in time for Old Westbend Weekend." She winced. "I've actually already taken some reservations for that weekend, so I don't really have a choice. It has to get done."

Two and a half weeks. Wow. Evan didn't know exactly what Addie was up against, but he could imagine it would take some elbow grease.

"I assume you'll have help."

Her head quirked, questioning. She was married, wasn't she? The Addie he knew wouldn't just hook up with someone. Granted, they were a bad example of that, but he'd always known her heart was much more conservative than they'd acted back then. They'd been teenagers—young and in love and stupid and careless. A winning combination. "I mean your husband. He must have some remodeling skills." Especially if they'd taken on a project of this magnitude.

"Actually, I'm divorced." The wounding that

flashed on her face cut into his chest with a dull butter knife.

Over the years, despite how things had ended, he'd always held a soft spot in his heart for Addie. He'd hoped and prayed for good things for her—especially once he'd gotten over his anger at God and started talking to Him again. But in all his wondering of what had become of her, he'd never imagined this. Never imagined she'd be broken and bruised at twenty-six years old.

His sympathies flared, and that *Don't get attached/don't get involved* mantra he'd been following since he'd arrived in town shot into the red zone. Addie was a once upon a time. A representation of what used to be. He was here for his mom…to get her place ready to sell, to honor her life somehow—whenever he figured out a way to do that—and to keep his existence as it was. With ten degrees of separation and a world to explore.

Addie, though she tugged on his heartstrings, didn't have anything to do with any of those.

Evan's face registered with all that Addie Ricci felt over her situation—concern, disappointment, surprise.

She had never planned to end up here. Divorced. Raising a child on her own. A decade of guilt and so much shame strapped to her back as a constant companion. And yet, the school bus of life had driven up, swung open the door and dumped her out on her rear end.

"I'm fixing things up on my own." The confession, as always, sent fear pulsing through her. What was she thinking? What was she doing taking on a project like this by herself? Believing she could run the B & B when she had no business training? She'd only stayed with Tito and Tita over three summers. Her mom's older cousin and her husband had loved on Addie like she was a daughter. They'd always talked about her growing up to run the B & B someday. That dream had been planted in Addie from a young age. But with Tito's sickness, things hadn't gone as planned.

They'd left Addie a small inheritance, and she'd saved it. The minute there'd been even a whisper of the B & B coming back on the market, Addie had launched her plan into action. She'd used the money for her down payment, and here she was, completely out of her league and determined beyond logic.

Those summers in Colorado had been the best of her life. Addie had loved the small town of Westbend and the opportunity to explore at will. Helping out with guests, answering phones, taking reservations, serving breakfast. Even cleaning rooms had been fun because it had all been a novelty to her.

That last summer in Westbend, she'd been less of a help, no doubt, because she'd been completely infatuated with the boy in front of her. Evan Hawke had been all sorts of temptation. Lean and muscular—he'd been riding bulls at the time, which had only added to his appeal. A bit of a risk taker, but when she'd gotten to know him, completely kind down to the marrow of his bones.

She'd loved him fiercely.

In the last ten years, Evan had changed from a boy into a man. Especially with that close-trimmed chestnut beard. His face, his shoulders, his build had all become more defined. The surge of attraction and interest Addie had experienced as a teenager stirred inside her even though Evan was the most off-limits of all the guys in the world.

"The last time I saw you…" The last time Addie had seen Evan, he'd been laid out in a hospital bed, frightened and lost, enduring excruciating pain. The night Addie had convinced Tita and Tito to let her sleep in the chair next to his hospital bed so that his mom could get some rest had been agonizing. When all of the busyness of the doctors and medical staff and family and friends had faded, Evan had been left with only the agony from his amputation. He'd writhed and cried out, and she hadn't been able to do anything to make it better except beg the nurses for more medication for him.

Evan rubbed a hand over his whiskered chin, the emotion she experienced at the memories seeming to surface for him too. "Yeah. That was the worst week of my life. And you stayed with me through it."

"Of course." Addie had always known that Evan had been distracted the day of his accident because of her. Staying beside him, supporting him—she hadn't wanted to be anywhere else. And when she'd had to go home to Michigan while Evan was still recovering and in shock... that had ripped a gaping hole in her chest.

The man in front of her now made that time and those memories seem as if they'd only existed in her imagination. His pants and shoe hid the results of the amputation that had taken his foot and lower portion of his leg so well that if she hadn't been present after his accident, she would never know a prosthesis hid beneath.

But of course it had all happened.

Including the aftermath. Their actions and his accident had contributed to a chain of events that Addie would never have imagined possible.

"And then you had to go home." Questions

brimmed in his eyes, a shade of brown that reminded her of her favorite coconut latte.

"Yes, I did." And things had spiraled out of control so quickly. Her parents had found out what she and Evan had been up to, and they'd cut off their relationship. Not with a trimmer, but with a sharp shovel, chopping straight at the root.

"But look at you now." She motioned to him. "All grown up and put together. Successful from what I hear." Just a few minutes in Evan's presence and she could sense his quiet self-assurance. He seemed at peace with himself in a way that Addie had been striving for since that time.

Reinstating the B & B was part of her attempt to reclaim her confidence, her life. To start over and leave the sins of her past behind. And yet one had just walked into the same store as her as a blatant reminder.

"Ah, I don't know about that." The tops of Evan's ears pinked endearingly. "So you and the little guy are on your own?" He nodded to Sawyer, who'd copped a seat on the floor. There the man went, changing the topic away from himself. He'd been like that as a teen too. Lots of guys liked to talk about themselves, but Evan had always focused on her, asking her a million questions about her childhood, the Filipino culture that made up her mom's side of the family, what her dreams were. Where she'd live if she could choose anywhere.

Those last two answers had been running the B & B and this town.

Addie's dreams might finally be waking up from a deep sleep, but she still had a long haul to actually make them feasible.

"Yep. Sawyer and I are a mom-and-son-superhero-crime-fighting duo." She paused. "But without the crime-fighting or superhero part." Her attempt at humor fell flat, ripping open the curtain into her personal torment.

"That has to be hard. I'm sorry, Addie." She could tell Evan was exactly that by the worried pucker that wedged between his eyebrows and the downward slope of his mouth.

She was sorry too. Sorry for the onslaught of painful, gut-wrenching memories that were choking her during this supposedly small talk conversation. Sorry for the mistakes she'd made that had led up to this moment. Sorry for what Evan didn't know and how it would most definitely hurt him.

"It's certainly not what I'd dreamed about or planned for." She acknowledged Evan's sympathy and shrugged as if her bad choices didn't matter, but of course they did. Adding a divorce to her *What was I thinking?* tally was embarrassing and excruciating. She should never have married Rex in the first place. He'd been a way to escape her parents, and the attempt had bombed, big-time. When she'd found out she was pregnant, their marriage had been over and done in a flash. Rex hadn't had any interest in becoming a father, or really, in her. "Sometimes life doesn't go like we expect it to." That was the understatement of the century.

"Mommy." Sawyer tugged on her leg. "We go."

"You're right, buddy. We do need to go."

The fact that Sawyer was still in the aisle with her was shocking. Asking any two-year-old boy—especially this one—to sit still or remain in one place for any amount of time was like asking a puppy not to have an accident on the carpet.

Addie's hands were full with a smattering of items Sawyer had "gifted" to her. She quickly placed them back in the correct spots. No need to destroy Herbert's while they were there. She was desperate for the people in this town to support her business and send referrals her way, not view her as incompetent.

"It was…good to see you, Evan." More lies. It was simply painful to see him. When a person had buried something for as long as she had, coming into contact with the initiating factor was like ramming repeatedly into a stone wall at top speeds.

"You too."

Addie scooped up Sawyer, retrieved her cart and headed for the checkout, her breathing shallow, her heart shredded into a thousand pieces of regret.

How many times had she begged a God she'd barely believed existed for an opportunity to share the truth with Evan? More than she could count. But what was she supposed to do? Blurt everything out in a hardware store? She didn't see that going well. And while Addie would happily shove off her shame and guilt and be free from the secrets, she couldn't get sidetracked either.

The B & B would require all of her energy and attention in the next couple of weeks. She *could not* fail. Her and Sawyer's livelihood depended on its success. So the fact that Evan Hawke had just walked back into her life was the biggest, most confusing wrench she could have imagined.

And she'd never been very good with mechanics.

## Chapter Two

"Did Misty have the baby?" Evan answered his phone over the hands-free device in his Subaru Forester and parked in exactly the same spot outside of Herbert's Hardware that he'd been in yesterday. The shock of seeing Addie must have messed with his logic, because after she'd taken off with Sawyer, he'd left too. With only half of the supplies he'd needed.

Addie had always been able to fry his mind like that eighties commercial of an egg depicting a brain on drugs. He just hadn't expected that she'd have the same effect on him after so much time.

"Nope. No signs of labor either." Christopher's frustration was evident. Evan's partner and friend was a trauma therapist who loved to adventure as much as he did. When they took groups out, Christopher was the counselor. The one who kept everyone from losing their minds. Who helped and nudged and listened. Christopher and his wife were due to have a baby three days ago, which was the reason the two of them had scheduled time off. They'd planned around her due date, not sure how else to handle things so that Christopher would most definitely be home when the baby arrived. But Evan was starting to realize babies didn't go according to schedule.

"We may need to extend our break," Christopher continued.

"Okay." Evan did the numbers. "We left ourselves some wiggle room before our first trip. We've got time. Don't stress. We'll figure things out. And if I have to take a group without you, that's okay too. I've listened in enough over the years. I could probably swing it." Not that he'd be anywhere near as good as Christopher. But Evan had been through his own trauma losing his leg. He knew the ins and outs of a shock like that. The ways it choked and stifled. The stark fear that followed up like a used-car salesman.

"Thanks, man. I'll keep you updated when we know more."

The two signed off.

Surprisingly, work at Evan's mom's house was going quickly. Unusual for a home project. Emotionally, it was a struggle for him to be inside those walls without his mom's chatter or laughter, so maybe that was why he was hurrying through the projects. Mom had developed heart failure after years of emphysema, and things had moved swiftly at the end, taking her down far before any of them had expected it to. They'd thought there was time, but like Addie had said yesterday, life didn't always go as planned.

Evan maneuvered out of the vehicle, this time leaving Belay in the backseat. The dog had FOMO, big-time, so she gave a pout and whine to let him know about her discontent before he shut the door. Evan shook his head and grinned. He'd left the windows cracked so she'd have plenty of air. The weather had warmed today, and it was supposed to reach sixty-six. Mud season was so sporadic in the mountains. Snowing one second, sun heating the ground the next.

After grabbing what he needed, Evan checked out and then loaded supplies into the back of his vehicle. He rolled down the windows as they drove through town, and Belay traveled from one side of the backseat to the other every few seconds to check things out. When he reached the turn that would take him back to Mom's house, he paused, stuck in the middle of the road as curiosity over Addie gripped him.

How was the remodel going? Was she buried under a mountain of projects or flying through them?

Ever since Addie had returned to Michigan and her parents at the end of that summer, Evan had wondered about where she'd ended up—about how her life had turned out. They'd kept up communication for about a week, texting or calling each other, but after that, her parents had effectively ended things between them. Addie had sent him a message about how her parents wanted her to concentrate on school, not on him. And that they needed to take a break from talking to each other.

Evan had understood at the time. He'd been a mess anyway, so focusing on getting better was a good idea for him. But when he'd tried to contact Addie in the months after that, just as a friend, just to check in, her number had no longer been in service.

Before Addie had left Colorado—and before his accident—they'd been inseparable. He'd worked some, and so had she, but they'd also played. They'd gone to the hot springs. Kayaked. Spent time swimming and laying out at the pool. She'd watched him compete in the rodeo. Evan often looked back on that time with a sharp ache radiating through him. He'd definitely taken for granted how simple and carefree his life had been before his amputation. All of that had changed the morning of his accident—when Addie had told him she was afraid she might be pregnant. Days later, while he was still in the hospital, she'd said it had been a false alarm—*Thank You, God.* Evan had plenty of regrets about the behavior that had gotten them to that point. He should have known so much better. Mom had raised him to think before he acted. But all of that was in the past, and he couldn't go back and change any of it now. God's grace didn't pick and choose what it covered.

A horn sounded behind him. Evan gave an apologetic wave before quickly moving to the side to let the car pass.

*Go home. You know better than to get involved.*

Evan was a wanderer. He didn't commit, didn't stay in one place too long, didn't get attached. Jace had been younger, so maybe he didn't remember as clearly or painfully the years upon years their dad had chosen alcohol over them. But Evan had learned the lessons imparted by their old man well. Most fathers taught their kids how to fish or do math or ride a bike. Theirs had taught Evan to detach.

He pressed on the gas, and like a disobedient child, his vehicle turned toward Little Red

Hen Bed & Breakfast. Everything in Evan said it wasn't a smart decision, but nothing in him listened. Curiosity won with minimal effort.

The B & B was located on the edge of town—a few blocks west of Main Street—nestled in the foothills of the Rocky Mountains. It had been built when the town was first founded, so it had historical charm that anything new couldn't compete with. Evan hoped, for Addie's sake and that of her little boy, that she could get the place functioning again. Turn a profit. Make a life for the two of them.

Probably exactly what she hoped for too.

He drove by slowly, relieved when she wasn't outside. The house's paint wasn't chipping, but it had seen better days. He heard faint crying and pressed on the brake. Nothing. He must have imagined it.

*Waaaaaahaaa.* There it came again.

Belay scooted across the backseat and shoved half her body out the window to investigate.

"What is it, girl? Did you hear that too?"

Three barks answered. Evan was pretty sure that was a yes in dog speak.

He eased into the drive, now even more certain that the wailing continued. For all he knew, Sawyer was being disciplined and didn't like it, and Evan would look nosy and intrusive rolling in to interrupt. But he couldn't ignore the concern that had skyrocketed at that sound. And Belay was on high alert too, confirming his intuition. He parked, then let Belay out, and the two of them followed the crying to the side of the house. The porch wrapped around the left, and Evan walked that way, Belay nestled against his leg as was her habit.

Sawyer's face, bright red and sopped with tears, appeared through the slats of the porch railing. Trapped.

"Hey, buddy. Did you get stuck?" Evan kept his voice calm, reassuring, while assessing the situation. Where was Addie? And how had the boy wedged his head through the spindles in the first place? "Remember me? We saw each other yesterday at the hardware store. You had some cool tape in your hand." *Bue tape* according to the tot.

Sawyer didn't acknowledge his comment or him, but he did stop screaming. "Doggie." He watched Belay, who had settled herself just in front of the boy, below the porch on the ground. If she'd gone around to be next to him, Sawyer would have had to strain his neck to see her. Smart girl.

"My dog's name is Belay. She's a golden retriever." Evan forked over some other random tidbits about Belay to keep Sawyer distracted as he sidled up to the kid and checked out the situation. Based on the redness behind his ears, he'd already tried backing himself out numerous times. "Where's your mom, Sawyer?"

New tears formed. "Mommy." His lips wobbled. "I want Mommy." The last word was barely decipherable, it came out as such a wail.

Evan could kick himself. That had been a stupid thing for him to say. "We're going to find her in just a second. Right after I get you out of here." He had some supplies in the back of his vehicle. Would any of those help? "I'll be right back. I'm going—"

"No-no-no." Sawyer's stark fear whapped Evan in the chest. Poor kid was afraid Evan was abandoning him.

"I'm not leaving you, Sawyer. I'm going to come up there right next to you. I'm just going to take the stairs." Evan had already started moving while he was talking. He hurried over to the steps, then around to the portion of the porch where Sawyer was trapped. "See? I'm right here." He dropped to the wooden slats next to the boy. "Let's see what we can figure out." He tried moving Sawyer's head this way and that, tilting. Then he pushed and pulled on the wooden spindles to create extra space, but they didn't give. He could saw one spindle off, get him out that way.

Sawyer pushed back with his hands and head, then cried out.

"Don't do that, squirt. Just stay still. We'll figure something out. You're okay for now. I know it doesn't feel good, but you're safe. I'm going to get you out of there." Somehow.

Belay began barking, spinning in circles and generally causing a ruckus. After a few antics, she'd settle, then go at it again. Sawyer became completely captivated by the dog, and his sniffling slowed. He reached for Belay, turning his shoulder and slipping one hand through the spindle to get to her.

"Good girl, Belay!" Evan maneuvered to standing and hurried to the steps while Sawyer was distracted. In no time at all, he was back on the ground in front of the boy. Sawyer had slid his arm back inside the spindle, but if he could do it once…surely he could do it again. "Reach for Belay. She wants you to pet her. She loves it right behind the ears." Evan helped Sawyer glide his hand back through, then his shoulder, then turned him so that his hip and leg and the rest of his body could follow. Sure enough, the boy slipped right between the spindles and into Evan's arms. He was so relieved that he held on to him for a second, and in response, Sawyer laid his cheek against Evan's chest and gave a hefty shudder. It was the best bit of gratitude Evan had ever experienced—no words needed.

Just as fast, Sawyer squirmed to be let down. "Doggie."

Evan placed him on the ground, and Belay licked the tears from his face, making him giggle. For the kid, it was as if the whole fiasco had never happened. For Evan, not so much. How long had Sawyer been stuck? And where was Addie? Was she okay? What if she was injured inside the house somewhere?

"Let's go find your mom." Evan took a few steps, but the boy didn't leave the dog. "Belay, heel." She obeyed, which in turn had Sawyer trucking after her. At the front door, Evan considered leaving Belay outside, but she was doing such a good job of doting on Sawyer that he let it slide. Given the circumstances, he doubted Addie would care about a little dog hair.

The door had been left open, and Evan called out as the three of them tromped inside.

So much for not getting involved.

Addie thought she heard the faint shout of her name, but she had to be imagining things, because the front door to the B & B was locked up tight and no one was in the house but Sawyer. She'd stationed him in front of the TV with his favorite movie no less than fifteen minutes ago, a snack and his sippy cup within reach.

Mother of the year. But she hadn't wanted him in this nasty bathroom with her while she steam cleaned the tile and grout, hoping that somehow it would be enough to make the bathroom usable again. She didn't have the money to pay for it to be redone. And the upstairs bedrooms were still in disarray from the last owner, so she didn't want to park him in one of those either.

Thankfully the interim owner of the B & B had kept most of the furniture from when Tito Benji and Tita Alice had been in full operation, because Addie would never be able to furnish the place herself, and she liked the vintage pieces. She planned to move things around and make use of everything.

Her name sounded again, more clearly this time. She peeked out the window. It wasn't coming from outside. Addie hurried out of the bathroom that connected to the Moose Room and removed the mask that covered her mouth and nose.

"I'm up here." Footsteps made the ancient stairs creak, and a jingle of some sort accompanied the movement.

How had someone gotten in the house? What was happening? And was Sawyer okay? She peered over the stair railing to find Evan coming up, followed by a golden retriever, followed by Sawyer. Her son's cheeks were red and splotchy. Had Evan barreled his way into the B & B and scared Sawyer? What in the world was going on?

Addie rounded the railing as Sawyer beelined for her, passing Evan. She snatched him up as he reached the top of the stairs, cradling him in her arms.

"What's wrong? What happened?" He just nestled into her neck and hiccupped. Like he did when he'd been crying hard. "Evan, what are you doing here? How did you even get inside? The front door was locked." If she sounded shrill, sue her. Her heart was thrashing against her rib cage.

"I found Sawyer on the south side of the porch with his head stuck through the spindles, screaming up a storm."

Addie sank to a seat on the top step at that announcement, keeping Sawyer nestled in her lap. "How is that possible? I locked the front door. And I've only been up here for fifteen minutes." He must have escaped right away. Heat and mortification swirled and swallowed her whole. *I'm a horrible mother.* She dropped her forehead against Sawyer's. How could she not have known any of that was going on? The bathroom window had been open, but he'd been on the other side of the house and the tool she'd been using had likely drowned out any chance of her hearing his cries.

She looked careless. Unfit.

The dog nestled against her, nudging into her legs, nosing Sawyer, comforting.

"Belay, no." Evan reached for the golden's collar, but Addie waved his hand away.

"She's fine." Addie buried fingers in the dog's soft fur, welcoming the flash of comfort. "Thank you for rescuing him." She met Evan's gaze for a millisecond before letting her lids close against the panic.

What if Sawyer hadn't gotten waylaid on the porch and had wandered farther from the house? Would they have even been able to find him in the wooded area that surrounded the B & B? There were dropping temperatures at night, plus wild animals. Addie shuddered at the horrible scenarios flipping through her mind.

"Sawyer, you can't go outside without Mommy." It was hard not to take her embarrassment out on him. Not to bark at him for escaping—especially when he could have seriously injured himself. Or worse. Panic turned her pulse into butterfly wings. "When I tell you to stay watching a movie, you need to do that. It's disobeying to go outside. And now you're going to lose your tablet time for later because you didn't listen to Mommy."

Fat tears slid down his cheeks as those big eyes implored her for grace. "I sorry, Mommy. I sorry."

"I know, bug. And I forgive you, but you still have to lose a privilege when you disobey. That also doesn't change the fact that I love you. Always. No matter what."

"I don't wanna lose a pribilege."

Addie either. Sawyer wasn't the only one who paid the price when he lost electronic time. It was a punishment for her too. That was the only part of the day she had to deal with paperwork for the bed-and-breakfast. And—as if she didn't have enough on her plate to worry about—now her son was turning into an escape artist. The kid was too adventurous for his own good. Reminded her of another male she knew. The one still standing in front of them. The one who led expeditions for a living and risked his life more often than she ever wanted to know about. Despite the fact that Addie had no right to think or care about Evan *ever*, she still broke that rule on occasion.

She wasn't the best at praying, but she'd asked for protection for Evan whenever he came to mind. Maybe that was because he was the first boy she'd loved. Or maybe it was because Evan was the father of her first child. The baby she'd held only once. The one who was being raised by adoptive parents. The one Evan didn't know anything about because Addie's parents had demanded as much.

*What are you doing here, Evan? Is this some sort of opportunity from God to tell you everything? Or have you simply waltzed back into my life to remind me of what all I've done wrong?*

If the latter was the case, Addie could free him from the job. She didn't have any problems remembering any of it all on her own.

# Chapter Three

At Sawyer's declaration that he was hungry—
he'd obviously gotten over the ordeal already—
Addie popped up from her perch on the stair and
brushed by Evan, the sweet scent of ripe summer strawberries traveling with her.

He and Belay followed her to the kitchen,
that same curiosity that had made him turn toward the B & B causing him to stay put when
he could easily let himself out the door.

Addie squeezed Sawyer so tight that he complained and squirmed. "Sorry-not-sorry, mister.
You owe Mom lots of hugs for what you just
put me through. Even if I did find out about it
after the fact."

Evan paused inside the large square opening
that separated the kitchen from the entrance to
the house and leaned against the frame. "He
must have watched you lock the door before

going upstairs while contemplating how to undo what you did."

Addie shuddered. "Scary on so many levels." She settled her forehead against Sawyer's. "Don't ever, ever, ever do that again. Pease." Her gaze met Evan's then, a smile surfacing. "Sawyer's version of *please*," she explained. "He always makes it sound like the vegetable. And since the majority of my conversations are at toddler levels, I tend to speak his language sometimes."

Addie could be losing her mind right now with Sawyer, or definitely her temper, but she was handling his escape with calm. At least on the outside.

"I think they make childproof locks for doors, don't they? Otherwise I could help you rig something up."

"They do. I can order online, or maybe Herbert's will have something."

"If you need help, let me know." *Remember you're not here to reinsert yourself into Addie's life, Hawke.* And yet a quick drive by had turned into a rescue and a continued conversation.

Addie plunked Sawyer onto the bench that lined the breakfast nook. The seat was under the windows at the front of the house.

"Would you like something to drink, Evan?" She opened the fridge. "I have…water. Or milk."

Her mouth tugged to one side and her shoulders inched up. "Sorry. We're operating at necessity levels around here."

"No, thanks. I'm good."

The countertops were missing from the cabinets, leaving the empty lower drawers open on the top. A small metal island cut down the middle of the kitchen, the underneath portion creating extra storage for hanging pots and pans, just like when Evan had visited the B & B with Addie as a teen. Not that much had changed with the place. A quick scan while they'd been upstairs told him that the interim owners hadn't demolished walls or changed the floor plan. Probably a good thing. Less for Addie to put back together.

"Are you sure? I'd like to reward you with something for saving my son's life."

Her curved lips hollowed out his stomach. Addie had been pretty in high school. She was beautiful now. "He wasn't really in huge danger. Just stuck."

"But he could have been if he'd gotten any farther." Her exasperated—likely fear driven—huff filled the kitchen. She gave Sawyer some crackers on a paper towel, half a banana and milk in a cup with a cover. "Not that I'm not grateful, but how did you end up driving by when you did?"

Evan shifted uncomfortably, moving his weight from his transtibial-amputation leg to his right. How to answer that?

"Oh no. Did you hurt yourself helping Sawyer?" Her concern was laser focused on his left leg.

And…that's what not answering right away got him. "No, no. I'm fine. I was…" *Spying. Too curious for my own good.* "I'd wanted to check out the place. See how the remodeling was going."

Addie returned the milk to the refrigerator. "I don't know that I'd call it a remodel. I'd like to do more, but I'm mostly finishing what the last owners started. And fixing up a few things, I guess." She leaned back against the cabinets opposite of Evan, facing him. "I'm more giving it a makeover. A facelift. Some Botox here and there."

Evan had eased farther into the kitchen during their conversation and now inspected the stripped cupboards, which were missing the doors.

"I'm planning to paint those. The last people must have planned the same but didn't get to it. Nice that they were already stripped down for me."

"True. That's a lot of work."

"I already ordered new countertops. I would have loved granite, but that's not going to happen on my budget. So laminate it is. I think it's a viable choice because laminate countertops are so much nicer these days. At least that's what I'm telling myself."

Sounded like she was also giving herself a pep talk. "I'm sure it will look great in here, especially with the cupboards freshened up." Not that Addie could do all of what the place needed in two and a half weeks by herself. "You have someone helping you out? A contractor or handyman?" She'd said she was on her own at the store—as in divorced—but she could be hiring some help.

"No. I don't have the money for that. I'm planning to do the work myself. I can paint cabinets. I've watched enough videos online to figure it out." A wobble threaded through her attempt at confidence, and Evan's heart gave a thump of sympathy.

There was absolutely no way Addie could turn this place around in two and a half weeks. Absolutely no way guests could arrive for Old Westbend Weekend and find the B & B intact and ready. The wood floors were scratched and needed refinishing, the countertops had to be installed, the cabinets painted. And that was just what Evan had seen in a few seconds. Certainly Addie had a much longer list.

Seeing how Addie's life had unfolded, the unexpectedly painful twist she'd been dealt which had landed her and Sawyer on their own… Evan couldn't just ignore how tough things must be for her. How hard she was working to reopen the B & B and create a life for her and Sawyer in Westbend. Addie had obviously had a rough go of it. Not that Evan knew the details of her marriage and divorce, but he could fill in the blanks.

*Then help her.*

He wished the thought had come out of nowhere, but Evan knew exactly the source who would have said it if she were present: his mom.

He could hear her as if she were standing next to him. *Do what you know you should do, Evan Hawke.* Or, more likely, she wouldn't have even used words. One look and he'd have been done. Signed up. Committed.

Growing up, Evan's mom had basically been a single parent because their dad hadn't contributed to the family. Unless consuming alcohol counted as a career. Mom had worked a ton of hours, and she'd been consistent for Jace and him. She'd never complained about the way her life had turned out even though she'd had every right to.

The last time Evan had gotten to see her alive, she'd told him that she didn't want him or Jace to sit around moping or wasting time after she was gone. *Be grateful to be alive, honey. I don't have any regrets over my life. You don't need to either.* Their mom had been nothing if not tough and strong. A fighter.

Ever since she'd passed, Evan had been looking for opportunities to honor her life and not focus on her death.

Helping Addie could very easily fit that bill.

But was the tug in his gut currently jumping and demanding his attention really about what his mom would have wanted? Or about his long-lost relationship with Addie?

No. They'd been kids. It couldn't be that old attraction driving this boat. Besides, Evan didn't do relationships well. Every time he got close to someone, he ended up distancing himself when things got serious. And he would never do that to Addie and her son.

She was off-limits for him.

Which meant he should be able to help her out, pay the single-mom tax and move on.

Evan's eyes flared with disbelief, as if he wanted to tell her that her plans to get the B & B completed in time for Old Westbend Weekend were impossible. But Addie didn't have any desire to hear that kind of negativity...or logic. It *had* to be possible. She didn't have any other choices. She'd already taken reservations for the

Moose and Fox rooms for Old Westbend Weekend. The other two master suites were still open, but she was hoping to have them filled too. And then during Old Westbend Weekend, she'd start booking up for the rest of the summer. Once people knew Little Red Hen Bed & Breakfast was back in business. It would take time and effort to resurrect the place, but it would be worth it. Addie could build a legacy for Sawyer to inherit in this town. Running the B & B was what she'd always dreamed about doing. Now she just had to turn those dreams into reality.

Sawyer was sneaking Belay, who'd settled near his feet, pieces of his crackers, but Evan didn't seem to mind, so Addie didn't say anything either. As long as her son was alive, well and not wandering around lost in the woods outside, she could forgive a small infraction like sharing his snack.

"Addie, it's physically impossible for you to do all of this in that amount of time without help."

Sparks grew at Evan's intrusion, igniting, heating. "I can't hire anyone, Evan. I've used every last cent to move us here from Michigan and to invest in supplies for this place."

"When do your countertops come in? It would be easier if you had the cabinets painted before then."

"Supposed to be the end of this week." Addie sucked in one of those calming breaths that only worked on other people. Between Evan bringing up all she had to do for the B & B and her guilt over the son he didn't know about, Addie was about to go in search of a brown paper bag and indulge in a panic attack.

"And then I assume you have a list of everything else you need or want done?"

Wants weren't on the list, but more needs than she knew how to handle were. She held up the sheet currently tossed into a drawer that was open and missing the countertop. She'd scribbled notes to herself all over it of what had to get done. Every time she saw the paper, dread squeezed her windpipe. Numerous things were crossed off but plenty remained.

"I can help you get some projects done around here while I'm in town. I'll have free time in between stuff at my mom's, and I don't have that much left to do there. I'm sticking around while the house gets shown and we see if anyone puts in an offer. Plus Jace is studying and training right now, so it's not like I can hang out with him as much as I'd like to."

Addie blinked. Evan was offering to help her out? Why? And how could she accept something like that when he didn't know she had been pregnant that summer? When he didn't know about their son?

"That's very generous of you, but I can't accept."

"Is this about me? About the leg? Because I promise to keep it under wraps."

"Please, Evan." Is that what not keeping in touch after she'd left town had made him think? Because that was nowhere near the truth. "Of course it's not about your leg. Never in a million years." How could he think she cared about something like that? Especially when she'd no doubt been a part of what had caused his run-in with the mower. "Do you ever…blame me for what happened?"

Evan's forehead quirked. "What? No. Of course not."

"But if I hadn't told you that morning…"

The morning of his accident, Addie had told Evan she was afraid she could be pregnant. Maybe she should have kept that information to herself, but she'd been panicking. Big-time. Her parents were so strict. She'd been certain they would lose it if they found out what she'd been up to. That she fancied herself in love with Evan.

She and Evan had both been frightened out of their minds.

He'd been distracted while mowing that day. He hadn't shut the machine off when he should have. It had rolled…

Addie swallowed the wave of sickness that squeezed her stomach in a fist.

"We were kids, Addie. I should have been paying better attention. And we shouldn't have been doing what we'd been doing in the first place. I'd never meant to…" Evan shook his head, regret evident. "I'm sorry for my part in that."

Addie had spent plenty of time dwelling on those misgivings over the years. "Me too." Neither of them had ever intended for things to go as far as they had, and there was no time machine to go back and change it now.

Just like she couldn't go back and keep herself from comforting Evan with a protective lie that would forever haunt her.

He'd been in so much pain and shock after the accident. Addie hadn't known what to do, how to help. He'd been in and out of it from the medication. So angry. Struggling beyond belief. The boy she'd loved had been replaced by one who shuffled through every emotional state minute by minute. Evan could barely function. How could he help her cope with a pregnancy scare?

That's why, a few days after the accident, when he'd asked her if there'd been any developments, she'd told him she wasn't pregnant. That it had been a false alarm.

He'd been so relieved that he'd hugged her,

wept into her shoulder. *Thank You, God*, he'd whispered over and over.

The fib had been temporary and not meant to be malicious. Addie had assumed she *would* get her period. That stress was just holding it captive. She'd been mad at herself for sharing that news with Evan in the first place. Angry that she'd no doubt been part of what had caused his accident.

Even if he was saying differently now.

Telling Evan that she wasn't pregnant had worked. In the days following, his emotional health had improved greatly. He'd started asking questions about mobility and the future. The dark circles had begun to fade away under his eyes.

When she'd returned to Michigan, there'd still been no sign of Aunt Flo, but Addie had refused to take a test, to confirm her fears.

She'd arrived home absolutely petrified.

At her parents' house, she'd started throwing up in the mornings. It had taken her mom less than a week to figure out what was going on.

Her parents had come up with a plan and dictated all of her next steps. When she'd said they needed to tell Evan the truth—that he could handle it once he was more removed from the accident—they'd disagreed.

They'd controlled everything: her care, preventing her from having any contact with Evan, homeschooling so that she could keep up with her junior year while pregnant, the adoption paperwork. She still wasn't sure how they'd managed the adoption without Evan's permission. Without his signature.

Addie had never asked. She was afraid to find out what they'd said or done in order to make that happen.

"I don't know what it is with everyone trying to shoulder the blame for my accident. Jace did the same thing, thinking it was his fault. It wasn't, just like it's not yours. I've long ago dealt with all that happened and my part in it. I can even say that I wouldn't be who I am today without the accident. Took me a few years to figure things out, but eventually, I did."

"Your work…" Addie studied him. "The fact that you help other people, that you provide a way for them to embrace life after they've been through a trauma…it's impressive, Evan."

"Thanks. It just kind of worked out that way." Now he looked like he wanted to crawl under the breakfast-nook table. He'd never been very good at taking a compliment or being the center of attention. Back when he'd been bull riding, he'd told her that he would block out the crowd when he competed. It had just been him and the bull in that arena for eight seconds. "In the beginning, I was focused on proving I could still do everything with one leg and a prosthesis. Other people got wind of what I was up to and wanted in. Things steamrolled from there. It's a God thing that I get to do what I love and help people at the same time."

What Evan had created from his hardship was the thing Addie found most attractive about him.

"All done, Mommy." Sawyer crawled across the bench seat of the breakfast nook and then curled arms around Addie's legs. More like he'd run out of snacks to toss to the dog.

Addie scooped him up. "I think Sawyer's spent from his ordeal." She ran a hand over his hair and followed it up with the press of her lips. "I should get him down for his nap."

The two of them were staying in the first-floor bedroom located behind the kitchen. Eventually she'd get the two-bedroom cottage out back livable, and she and Sawyer would occupy it. Addie had considered including it as a rental unit, but she'd done the math, and as long as she ran at full occupancy during mapped-out times of the year, they'd be fine. And she wanted to provide Sawyer with a place that was just theirs, away from guests every moment of the day. She'd add the main-floor bedroom to the rental list once she and Sawyer moved into the cottage, though she wasn't going to rush that stage or renovations. As Evan had pointed out—and she already knew—she had a lot on her plate.

"I should take off anyway, but I'll swing by tomorrow afternoon and help you paint the cabinets."

"There's no need—"

"Addie." Evan cut her off, but his soft tone curled around her heart, warm and tempting and absolutely off-limits. "I've got extra time and you need help. There's no denying it."

She opened her mouth. Closed it. He was right. She couldn't deny it.

"My mom…she worked so hard." Evan continued. "She did most everything on her own, despite my dad. But once in a while, someone would give her a leg up. A barely used bike would be handed down for me or Jace. Clothes. Even the occasional meal would get dropped off by someone well-meaning. Jace was younger, so maybe he didn't notice all of those details. But I did. Every single time." Evan cleared his throat, moisture glistening in those toffee eyes of his. "I'm not saying we were the poorest of the poor, but we certainly weren't rich either. We always had something to eat, but I don't remember things being easy. I was old enough to hear details, to read between the lines. I understood far more than I let on, but I stayed out of it because I didn't want to upset my mom."

Addie swallowed the rush of sympathy filling her throat. She'd known enough about Evan when they were teens to piece most of that together but hearing it from him now made it that much more real.

"After my amputation, I went out to the hot springs with some friends wearing my post-op cast. It was too far for me to be going at that point. Stupid, really, but I'd just wanted to feel normal. To be one of the guys again. I ended up reinjuring myself, splitting open some stitches. Recovering from that was awful, and I had to wait longer to get my prosthesis. All because I'd been so determined to do something on my own time and schedule. My own strength."

He thought she was doing the same—refusing because of some stubborn determination to handle the B & B on her own—but she wasn't. What was she supposed to say? It wasn't about not being able to accept help. It was that she had the power to hurt Evan immensely with the information she held. And the power to make the man loathe her for keeping it from him. It was that every moment around him reminded her of what she'd done—what her parents had forced her to do. And yet it all still felt like her fault. Her sin to atone for.

"Evan. I'm sorry."

"I'm over it now. But I'm just saying…don't be me. Don't be stubborn. Let me help you."

"I can't give you anything in return." Her voice hollowed at that admission. She'd risked everything to reopen the B & B. Sawyer's future and their livelihood hinged on it. Addie didn't have any money to spare.

"I'm not asking for anything. Just a way to honor my mom. To do what she would have wanted me to do."

A huff of air escaped from Addie. "You make it hard for a girl to say no, Evan."

"Then don't. My partner's wife is having a baby, so we scheduled out a few weeks without trips. I have the time to help out, and I have no doubt you need it." Sympathy radiated from him with the last comment, softening the blow.

Of course she did. Anyone could see that. And if Addie kept fighting him, Evan would just grow curious as to why.

If he insisted on helping her at the B & B, then Addie could use the time spent with him to figure out a way to tell him about their son. Maybe Evan offering his assistance was a gift from God. An answer to jilted, broken prayers and a chance to tell him the truth and wipe her slate clean.

Addie would love nothing more.

## Chapter Four

❧

"Come on, bugaboo." Addie picked up the canvas tote full of library items that would hopefully occupy Sawyer while she worked on the B & B. She held open the library door, and Sawyer abandoned the puzzle he'd been playing with.

Outside, spring sunshine smiled down on them. The weather was in the sixties, but the heat from the sun made it feel warmer. Cheery yellow flowers bloomed on the bushes that lined the library path, and the mountains, which still held a glittering layer of snow, rose up in the west.

Once again, Sawyer took off like a lightning bolt. He quickly shot up the sidewalk, and panic pulsed through her veins. If she called out to him and then ran to catch up, he'd probably consider it a game and take off.

She jogged after him quietly, the canvas tote

of books and DVDs banging against her leg. At the last second she snagged his hand, preventing him from tumbling into the street, her heart thundering like horse hooves. In the last month, he'd suddenly become much faster at breaking away than he used to be. Addie hadn't adjusted to the change yet, and Sawyer wasn't leaving her any time for a learning curve.

She knelt beside him. "Sawyer, the street is dangerous. You have to stay by me. Cars won't be able to see you if you run out there, and you'll get hurt."

"Owie?"

"Yes. Big, big owie." She stood, a tight grip on his hand. "Let's go find Evan."

"Eban, Eban." Sawyer repeated with cheer. Since the man had rescued him yesterday, Sawyer had decided they were best buds.

It was just the extra helping of guilt Addie needed in her day.

What had she done?

She'd been asking herself the same question for the last twenty hours but had yet to come up with any helpful answers. Accepting Evan's help was not her smartest move. It was like working with the enemy—at least from his perspective.

Before Evan had left the B & B yesterday, they'd exchanged phone numbers, and by text last night he'd offered her some leftover paint he had from working at his mom's. It was almost a full gallon of ivory—exactly what she needed in order to freshen up the Fox Room. Addie couldn't refuse a gift like that right now, even if everything in her was screaming that she should.

With her plans to hit the library right when it opened this morning and his appointment with Jace and their Realtor at The Fork and Spoon, they'd decided to meet up in town so she could grab the paint. Maybe she'd even get a coat done this morning.

And maybe she'd suddenly turn into a gifted opera singer.

Addie's throat tightened at the reminder of all she had left to do on the B & B. Yes, Evan planned to help her, but his assistance came with copious amounts of heavy emotional baggage. For all she knew, the remorse strapped to her back might actually slow her progress down instead of making projects go faster.

When they reached The Fork and Spoon, an elderly couple was leaving, so Addie held the door open for them to exit. Sawyer took the opportunity to stream inside, and a worn-out breath swelled and spilled from her.

At least he couldn't get run over by any traffic in the small space.

Inside, Evan was sitting on one of the circular

rotating stools that lined the breakfast counter, and Sawyer was attempting to climb the open one next to him.

"Hey, Sawyer." Evan greeted her son, content to let him figure out how to get onto the stool himself. Once he did, the two fist-bumped. Addie wasn't sure they should be celebrating Sawyer conquering any new physical frontiers. She needed him to slow down and do less right now, not more.

"Addie." Evan lifted his coffee mug in greeting, those caramel eyes meeting hers. A ping of awareness shot through her.

"Morning." The word croaked out like she hadn't spoken to anyone yet today, which wasn't true. Evan somehow just sent her straight back into teenage-girl mode. Squirrelly and awkward with a dash of off-limits pining thrown in just for torturous fun.

"You two want any breakfast? Want me to move down a stool? Make room?"

"No. Thanks. We'll just grab the paint and go."

"Okay." His head gave a questioning tilt. "You all right, Addie?"

He didn't fill in the rest, but she could improvise based on the concern puckering his brow. *You look frazzled and tired. Like you could use a month of vacation.*

All of those things were true, but none of them were fixable right now.

"I'm okay." Or at least she was trying to be.

"Pan-ake." Sawyer yelped out his little boy lingo for his favorite breakfast, eyed Evan's plate and smacked his lips.

"I promise I fed him this morning." Instant oatmeal, which was nowhere near as good as The Fork and Spoon's pancakes, but Addie had been operating as minimally as possible, including meals and dishes.

Evan tore a strip of pancake from the side of his plate. "Can I give him this?"

"Sure." She'd barely answered before Sawyer yanked the piece out of Evan's hand and wolfed it down.

"Are you sure you fed this kid?"

"I'm sure. Sometimes it feels like an on-the-hour event. I don't know how he can eat so much."

"Just wait until he's a teenager." Good memories tugged at Evan's mouth. "Mom was always talking about how much food Jace and I could put away."

Addie wasn't ready to go there yet. She couldn't even handle *today*, let alone the future.

Everything was crowding in on her—Sawyer's antics, finding a way to tell Evan about Eli, the B & B. Addie was going to have a breakdown right here in the middle of The Fork and Spoon with half the town watching.

Even with Evan's help, she had way too much to do for the bed-and-breakfast, and she was starting to hyperventilate about the size of the project she'd undertaken. The project she'd used their nest egg to invest in. Addie could have saved the money from Tito and Tita. It could have provided a cushion for her and Sawyer. Instead she'd gone all in on the B & B. It was a calculated risk, yes, but it was still a huge one.

Which was why she'd pushed to do the renovations so fast. She needed the money from guests to come in quickly so it could cover the operating costs.

What if she'd risked everything in order to provide a future for Sawyer, and she ended up doing the exact opposite? Landing them on the street without a job or home?

The last owners hadn't fared well. Why had Addie believed things would somehow go easier for her?

"Whatever spinning ride you're on, you need to get off." Evan interrupted her downward tumble. "Sit down a second."

"I really can't. I've got to get back to the B & B." It wasn't just fixing and painting and cleaning she had to carve out time for. Addie also needed to restock—coffee, tea, soaps and shampoos, bathrobes for the rooms. People sought out those small touches, and Addie wanted to provide them. And she *had* to get everything perfect right away so that guests could leave raving reviews. The B & B would drown without five-star recommendations.

"How am I going to get good reviews if everything isn't running smoothly? What have I done?"

"Okay, that's enough." Evan took the library bag from her, set it on the floor by Sawyer's stool, then tugged on her hand until she plopped to a seat on the open stool to his left.

Bossy.

"Coffee or tea?" he asked. "It's on me."

"I don't have time for either."

"I'm afraid you're about to pass out. Which is it?"

"Coffee. With cream and sugar." *Great job holding out, Addie. First you accepted Evan's help on the B & B. Now this. Next he'll offer to marry you and you'll say yes to that too.*

But Evan was right—she did need to sit. Her breathing was coming in short, shallow spurts, and for a second, her vision had blurred.

"Shorty," Evan called out to the lean, over-six-foot man behind the counter. "Can we get a cup of coffee over here?" Shorty gave a nod and then turned and filled a mug that held the logo for a local children's clothing store. He set it in front of Addie, then pushed the cream and sugar her way.

"Sure you don't want anything else? Some breakfast?" Evan's offer was kind, but she waved it away.

"No, thanks. I'm good. Thank you, Shorty." On the rare occasion that Tito had taken her out for breakfast, they'd always come to The Fork and Spoon. Shorty had been working here then. The man was a fixture behind the breakfast counter, though he rarely talked. Only said what was necessary and not even that if a gesture would suffice. Shorty had always been short on words and long on height.

Addie doctored her coffee and Evan gave her a second to settle, continuing to parcel out squares of pancake to Sawyer.

"You can eat your own breakfast, you know. I can get him a pancake. Or a replacement for yours."

"I was pretty much done." Evan patted his flat stomach. "I definitely needed to be. I'd already eaten two of them myself."

She raised an eyebrow. "Watching your figure?"

"Something like that. Working on the house is physical, but it's not the same as what I'm used to. I feel like my body has already begun changing in the last week."

"You turned your mom's house around that fast?" Dread squeezed her lungs. She was moving too slowly. The B & B would never get done at this pace. How would she ever—

"And I see you just got back on the panic ride."

Her mouth slid into a reluctant curve as she took a sip of coffee. "Am I that obvious?"

"It's like you have Currently Freaking Out plastered across your forehead."

"Perfect."

"My mom's house isn't done yet, if that helps you at all. And the projects there aren't nearly as big as your place. I'm not remodeling the kitchen. I'm just tiling a bathroom and replacing some windows. I redid some trim. Painted. Little things."

"It's nice of you to try to make me feel better."

"Is it working?"

"No."

He laughed—a quiet, pleasant sound that had been filed away in her memories in a box labeled Good But Don't Open. Some things just stung too much when they were unpacked.

Sawyer was practically in Evan's lap now, reaching for the remaining pieces of pancake that Evan had cut. Instead of resituating him on his own stool, Evan scooped Sawyer up and settled him on his lap. A chunk of Addie's heart crashed to the floor and shattered.

*That could have been our son.*

*No, it couldn't have. You were barely seventeen when you gave birth. The life he has now is so much better than anything you could have provided.*

Men seemed to fall into one of two camps with kids—completely out of their element or comfortable because they had children of their own. Evan didn't fit either of those categories. At least, not that he knew about.

Guilt shot up her throat like acid reflux.

Addie had always wanted to tell Evan about Eli…to stop the terrible lie from continuing. Every year on their son's birthday, she wrote Evan a letter. And every year she didn't send it.

Because how do you tell a man that he has a son he doesn't know about? How do you tell him that you'd been a wuss and should have stood up to your parents, but you didn't know how?

Addie's parents had threatened to cut her off and kick her out of the house if she communicated with Evan in any way, shape or form. They'd been so angry and disappointed about the unplanned pregnancy, and they'd blamed Evan for his part in all of it. Addie could have reached out to Evan despite their threats, but how could two teenagers have made that scenario work? Especially in the aftermath of Evan's trauma. It wasn't like he would have just been able to get any old job and support her and a baby.

She'd been sixteen at the time. Going against her parents would have landed Addie pregnant and on her own, without a job or way to support herself and without medical care for the child she was carrying.

She really hadn't had a choice.

She'd chosen to bring a healthy baby into the world so that more equipped parents could raise and love him. She'd chosen to stay silent for their son's sake.

Evan's phone chimed, and he checked it, a huge grin stretching his features. *Sweet peas*, the man was gorgeous when he smiled like that. The curve of his mouth perfectly matched their son's. Addie knew because the only thing her mom and dad hadn't been able to take from her was the communication Eli's adoptive parents sent her every year on or around his birthday. They included updates and pictures that showed him happy and laughing and so, so full of life. Opening that envelope each year was equal parts solace and agony.

"Good news, I take it?"

"My partner, Christopher, and his wife had their baby. A little girl." He showed her a picture of a newborn wrapped in a hospital blanket, wrinkled face, dark hair, lids shuttered, cheeks that would make a grandmother swoon.

"Precious."

"I was starting to wonder if she was ever going to arrive."

"Babies have a way of making an entrance." She'd gone over her due date with Eli too, but Sawyer had been right on the money.

"I'm glad he'll be able to use the time off to actually be with his daughter now. We have a group scheduled about two and a half weeks out. Hopefully that's enough time for his wife to get the hang of things. I can do the trip without him, but I'd prefer not to."

"There's never enough time to adjust to a baby, but I'm sure she'll handle it well. And you're planning to stay in town until then?"

"Yeah. I'd like to see Jace as much as I can in between his studying and training. I still have a few things to do on the house, depending on what the Realtor says today. And if it doesn't sell while I'm here, Jace and I are going to rent it out for the time being. So I'm planning to take care of those details while I'm in town."

Which meant Addie not only had two weeks remaining to get the B & B functioning and ready for guests, she also had about that much time to figure out a way to tell Evan about Eli. Because after that, he'd be leaving town again.

And this time, she was determined that he'd go knowing the truth.

Addie's cheeks had pinked with color—finally—but she hadn't completely lost the panic she'd been wearing when she walked inside. Maybe she wouldn't until the B & B projects were done.

"It's all going to work out, Addie."

"Easy for you to say." She gave a pitiful sigh and took a long sip of coffee.

"Plus, thanks to a handsome, strapping young lad who's going to help you out, you won't be completely on your own."

She blinked in mock surprise. "You're calling in a friend? How generous!"

Humor surfaced. "You know, I could easily find some more projects to complete at my mom's and take up more of my time."

"That's not necessary!" Her head shook quickly. "If you're determined to honor your mother by helping me out, I could never be so cruel as to take that opportunity from you."

"Ah. I see. How generous of you."

"That's why I took such a risk reopening the B & B." She turned serious, staring into her coffee cup, swirling the liquid. "It's what Tito and Tita always wanted. And me too. It was a good opportunity to create something I can pass down to Sawyer, but also, I just couldn't resist this way to honor them and what they meant to me. They didn't have children of their own, and they always treated me like a daughter. Better than my own parents, really."

"I'm sorry." Evan had known Addie's relationship with her parents had been tense when she was a teen. He was sad to hear that had continued, and yet, at the same time, he understood it. Evan had loved his dad in a way that only a kid could—despite his actions. If he'd lived, they would no doubt have a tumultuous relationship of their own to bog through.

Sawyer downed another bite of pancake and made a smacking sound of approval. Evan grinned at him. "Pretty good, right? The Fork and Spoon makes the best pancakes." His gaze switched to Addie. "Sometimes when I'm freezing and climbing, I imagine myself sitting right here."

"For me it was always at Tita's table. She made the best breakfasts. Especially *pandesal*." Evan groaned. The faintly sweet bread rolls were melt-in-your-mouth good. Evan knew because he'd gotten to experience them on more than one occasion.

"That's what you can pay me with for helping you out on the B & B."

*"Pandesal?"*

"Yes."

A slow smile surfaced from Addie. "Okay. You drive an easy bargain, Evan Hawke."

*And you drive a hard one, Adelyn Ricci.* Evan had signed up to help Addie for all the right reasons but keeping his thoughts in that direction and not on *her* would be harder than he'd originally realized.

He'd forgotten the havoc one of her smiles could cause. Or that her deep brown eyes were like sinkholes he fell right into and couldn't— or didn't want to—climb back out of.

"Evan Hawke!" A voice boomed from over his shoulder. "You're just the person I wanted to see." An older gentleman with a round waist wearing a button-up shirt and slacks approached, then greeted Evan with an enthusiastic whack on the back that caused him to lurch forward and the coffee in his hand to slosh over the side of his mug. Thankfully it landed on the countertop and not on Sawyer. The kiddo was too enthralled with the last of Evan's pancake to even notice the jostle.

Evan wiped the residual liquid from his fingers with a napkin. Should he remember this man? He did look vaguely familiar. Maybe someone from his childhood?

"Morning, sir." Evan offered his hand, and the man shook it with excitement.

"Bill Bronson," he said. "Mayor of Westbend."

That's where Evan recognized him from—the sign outside the courthouse included this man's mug. What would the mayor want with him? And how would he know Evan's name?

"We have a bit of an emergency," the mayor continued, "and I hear you're just the man to get us out of it."

"Oh?" Dread shot up Evan's spine like a weed after a week of rain. "I'm not going to be in town very long." *And just because I'm here doesn't mean I'm getting involved.* The Addie situation was about his mom. Evan was unwilling to go above or beyond that.

"Will you be here through Old Westbend Weekend?"

*Yes, but I'm not sure I want to admit that to you until I know what you're asking for.*

He went for evasive. "What do you need done, sir?"

"Call me Bill. And I need a hero."

Behind him, Addie snort-laughed, then tried to cover it up with a cough. She began humming that eighties song about needing a hero. Somehow Bill was oblivious to the connection to their current conversation.

Evan glanced over his shoulder. "Weren't you in a hurry to get the paint and go?"

Her amusement was unrepentant. "I can wait."

"I mean the town needs a hero," Bill continued when Evan turned back to him. The mayor's clarification still really wasn't helping. "We had someone lined up to be our hometown hero for Old Westbend Weekend. Darian Nickert—a war vet. Unfortunately he passed away last week, so now we need a fill-in."

"You need some suggestions of who could step in?" Evan hadn't been back much since he'd left town. He probably wouldn't be a great help.

Bill guffawed as if he'd made the funniest joke, one hand resting on the ledge of his Santa Claus stomach. "No, no. We want *you* to be the hero. People keep talking about what you do, how you help others. You're highly esteemed. Local. You're just the ticket."

"I'm not sure that I fit that description at all, sir. I think you've got the wrong guy."

"Please call me Bill. And we definitely disagree on that. I'm not taking no for an answer. Not until you think about it."

Too bad, because that was the response Evan planned to give. Westbend swarmed with people on that weekend. He would rather crawl under a rock than get up in front of them for any reason. If that was even what the hero thing entailed. Evan could ask, but that would show interest. And he wasn't interested in showing interest.

How could he tell the mayor that this wasn't

his town anymore? Evan had been gone too long. He'd become a wanderer, and he liked it that way.

It was…safer.

Putting down roots and letting people in just allowed for the opportunity for someone to come along and yank them out of the ground.

And Evan knew better than anyone how much that hurt.

# Chapter Five

Addie was straddling a fence between the fields of gratefulness and guilt, and she planned to hop down.

Soon.

Yesterday afternoon, she and Evan had knocked out painting the cabinet bases and doors. It had gone so much faster and better with his help. Then this morning the countertops had been delivered, and Evan had recruited his brother to help with the heavy lifting.

They'd needed him.

After Jace took off, they'd spent the day attaching the countertop to the cabinets, cutting it, filing, gluing. Through it all, Addie had been looking for the perfect opening to talk to Evan, to bring up the past.

She felt guilty as all get-out accepting his help without him knowing the truth. And if finding out made Evan take off and decide not to lend any more assistance, she could live with that.

She just couldn't live with the lie anymore.

Even if telling Evan about Eli was the hardest thing she'd ever had to do, she had to do it.

"I all done, Mommy. I all done." Sawyer dropped to the kitchen floor, proficient in dramatics. He'd spent the day playing with Belay and cycling through various activities Addie had suggested for him—dunking in a toddler basketball hoop out on the porch, Play-Doh, stickers, coloring. He had also succumbed to a nap at one point though he'd fought that option valiantly.

Addie had used a baby gate to block off the porch steps, confining Sawyer to either that space or the house throughout the day, and amazingly, that's where he'd stayed. Likely the props for that should go to Belay, Best Dog Ever and Toddler Whisperer Extraordinaire.

"Can you at least move yourself over to the booth by the breakfast nook?" Addie asked Sawyer. Not that that option was much better. It needed work too. But the kitchen floor was a mess. A definite construction zone.

He kicked his legs. "I don't wanna. Don't wanna, wanna, wanna." Belay nosed around the lump of crabby boy, licking Sawyer's knees that poked out of his shorts. Sawyer giggled but still didn't perk back up. Was he sick? Tired?

Addie knelt and checked his forehead. It was clammy, but in a running-around-all-day-need-a-bath kind of way. Not in a sick way.

Her phone dinged from its perch on the breakfast-nook table, and Addie stepped over Sawyer to check it.

"I got another reservation for Old Westbend weekend!" She yelped, and Evan popped out from under the kitchen sink, which he was re-installing.

"That's great."

"And they're staying all week." She did a happy dance, and Belay joined her, tail wagging, mouth grinning.

Evan laughed that low chuckle that did too many things to her insides before returning to his dark cave.

The reservation was a huge relief. A stress, too, because of what still needed to be done to the B & B, but like Evan had said, it would all work out. Somehow.

It had to.

The time on her phone read six thirty. Six thirty! Way past dinner time. No wonder Sawyer was a mess. He had to be starving. She usually fed him close to five o'clock and then another snack before an early bedtime.

"Mommy forgot to feed you, bugaboo." She stepped over Sawyer again. "Let me get you some food."

She rummaged in the fridge and found an orange. After making quick work of peeling it, she placed it on a paper plate and delivered it to the breakfast nook. She scooped Sawyer up, squeezing him before plunking him down on the bench.

Sawyer took the bait.

"I'll make some peanut-butter-and-jelly sandwiches for dinner too."

She thought that might earn a complaint since they ate plenty of them, but Sawyer just nodded as he inhaled the orange. How could she have forgotten to feed her kid? Addie was winning at all the things lately—mom or otherwise.

Belay, sweet soul, plopped down halfway under the table, next to Sawyer's constantly moving feet. The dog was the ultimate protector and companion. No wonder Evan took her everywhere. The last day and a half wouldn't have gone nearly as well without the golden to distract and entertain Sawyer.

Evan returned from the back where there was a small Dumpster.

"I feel like I should pay Belay for babysitting," Addie quipped.

The answering tilt of Evan's lips still had the

power to turn her insides round and round like a dryer drum. "I could say the same about Sawyer. Last night Belay was so exhausted she slept like a rock. Sawyer definitely wore her out in a good way."

She retrieved the jelly and peanut butter, snagged the bread and set it all on the island, which had been shoved to the side of the kitchen today.

*You should offer him something to eat.*

Evan had slaved away yesterday afternoon and again today at her bed-and-breakfast with nothing to show for it, yet the offer didn't slip from her tongue.

It wasn't that Addie didn't like spending time with Evan. She did. He was easy to be around. His quiet sense of humor made her laugh and his calm seeped into her pores, communicating that somehow, things would get done on time. That she hadn't thrown her and Sawyer's life away by attempting to reopen the B & B.

But liking him and wanting to be with him were definitely not on the menu. Not with all that had transpired between them. Every second with Evan was a ticking time bomb. A reminder of what he didn't know.

Still, she didn't have a choice but to feed him. Even though that wasn't nearly enough to thank him for his help. "Would you like a sandwich?

Peanut butter and jelly. I've got smooth peanut butter. Sorry, no crunchy." Her hands worked quickly, spreading the dark grape across the bread. "I know it's not much, but it's all I've got." A normal person would order a pizza, buy Evan some real dinner, but Addie didn't have extra funds for that. "Of course I understand if you have to go. If you have things to get to."

"Actually, that sounds really good. I haven't had a PB&J in a long time."

Funny. She and Sawyer ate them a couple times a week. Especially lately when she hadn't had time to cook. Once the B & B reopened, though, she'd be in the kitchen plenty.

She whipped up three plates, cutting Sawyer's sandwich into smaller sections, then added baby carrots and potato chips. Not exactly gourmet, but it would do.

Sawyer was still sitting on the bench, but he'd scooted toward the middle after finishing his orange. The dog was under the table, and Sawyer kept playing peekaboo with her.

Addie set his plate in front of him along with one for her and Evan on each side. The torn vinyl bench taunted her. *I know, I know. I'll get to you next. Or at least soon.*

"Food's ready," she called out to Evan.

"I'm going to turn the water back on so I can wash my hands."

Once he returned to the kitchen, he flipped on the water in the sink. They'd adhered it to the countertop earlier. It must be considered dry enough if Evan was using it now. Addie handed the paper towels to Evan for drying, then copied him.

They let Sawyer do the talking while they ate. He told them about the doggie, the butterfly they'd been chasing, the racing he and Belay had been doing. Still, he managed to finish much faster than either of them.

"All done." He showed Addie his empty plate like he'd won a prize.

"Good job. Do you want some more?"

His little head shook.

Sawyer climbed down from the bench, scooted under the table and caught up with Belay. They ran through the bottom floor of the house, Sawyer giggling, Belay with a perma-grin on her face, tail wagging a mile a minute, the click of her toenails skittering across the wood floors.

"I hope Belay isn't messing anything up. Let me know if you'd rather she be outside."

"What's there to mess up? I still need to refinish the hardwood floors." Addie waved a hand over the first floor of the house, which was a near-disaster zone—except for the fresh countertops and painted wooden shells waiting for dried cabinet doors to be reattached.

The kitchen already looked one-thousand-percent better. And she owed one thousand percent of that to Evan.

"If you hadn't helped me, I would be drowning right now. There's no way the kitchen would be so far along. Thank you."

He paused with a chip halfway to his mouth. "You're welcome."

The man should wear a superhero cape. "So are you considering what Bill Bronson asked about yesterday morning?"

Fear flashed in his eyes. "Ah, no. Definitely not."

"Why not?"

"Because there's not one part of me that feels qualified for something like that."

"But you are a hero. How many people have found a way to overcome their trauma by going on an expedition with you?" He remained silent. "You should at least think about it."

"Okay." He acquiesced and then got up, filling two plastic cups with water from the sink. He returned to the table and his seat, handing her one.

"Thanks." She took a sip. She hadn't done a great job of staying hydrated while working on the house. She needed to rectify that. She also might need to set a timer on her phone so that she actually remembered to feed her son. "That was a quick agreement with my suggestion."

"Mostly because I'm not planning to consider it, but I also don't want to argue." A grin followed the admission, and her traitor cells sighed in mutual adoration. Evan's looks were subtle. The kind that snuck up on a girl and made her fall deeper into like with each passing day. Or at least they had once upon a time.

His hair was longer than he'd kept it in high school. When Addie had first met him and he'd been riding bulls, it had been short. She'd loved the feel of the crisp cut under her fingertips. But now it was thick and almost wavy. The color of chestnuts. His eyes were brown, but while hers were molten chocolate cake, his were lighter, more taupe. He was also rocking enough scruff to sufficiently be labeled a beard, but it was trimmed short and neat.

Addie approved. She didn't want to, but there was no use fighting the inevitable. She'd always been attracted to Evan. That wasn't going to just disappear, even with the past drawing an invisible wedge between them.

Addie was lost in thought, and Evan would pay a hefty sum to know what was filtering through her mind. They'd worked together for a day and a half, but the conversation hadn't gone much beyond Sawyer or the B & B.

Though she had asked about his mom and listened intently as he'd recapped the end of her life. Addie had swept silent tears from her cheeks, and for a second, Evan had thought she was going to cross the room and wrap her arms around him, tuck under his chin just like she used to do when they were teens. It was as if the option flitted across her features, as easy to read as a children's book. But then instead of following through, she'd gone back to her task, leaving him hungry for exactly what he shouldn't and couldn't have.

Addie was off-limits. Especially with Sawyer involved. Evan ran from relationships when they got anything close to serious. Twice in his twenties, he'd begun dating someone great and ended up breaking things off, not because anything had been wrong, but because things had been too right. Who did that? Messed-up people, that's who.

Sawyer flew into the kitchen again, Belay on his heels. "Bel, sit," Sawyer commanded. Belay obeyed. "Good, girl! Let's be race cars!" Sawyer took off, making an engine sound, and Belay streaked after him.

"It's almost as if we don't even exist." Addie softened while watching Sawyer scoot around the corner. She was present again, the dark storm cloud from seconds before wiped clean.

"Unless he needs sustenance."

"Unless his mother forgets to feed him, you mean."

"I didn't notice what time it was either. You're not the only one."

"He did pretty great today, thanks to Belay."

Evan took a swig of water. "Thanks to you. You had plenty of tricks up your sleeve, things to keep him occupied. Does it always take so much to entertain him?" Evan had been shocked by how busy Sawyer was. The kid was the definition of unbridled energy. But Addie handled him like a pro. She'd fluctuated from helping with the countertops to making sure Sawyer was safe and entertained, all while making it look easy.

"Pretty much. I find that if I don't have something for him to do, he gets into trouble far too quickly."

"Sounds like a boy. And like something my mom would have said about Jace and me. He's a good kid, Addie."

"Thanks. I'm pretty partial to him." So much pain registered across Addie's features, it was like someone was hammering her bare foot to smithereens.

"Addie?"

"I—" Her mouth closed. Moisture rushed her pretty eyes and she blinked numerous times. "I might regret my relationship with Sawyer's dad, but I could never regret him. He's my everything."

Evan got the distinct impression she'd been about to say something else and changed her mind. But then, maybe his read on Addie was way off.

"I take it Sawyer's dad doesn't keep in contact with him?" He was curious about the man she'd married. Curious as to why she'd made that choice when it didn't sound like he'd been good to her.

A gaping emotional wound yawned wide and visible before she quickly stitched it shut. "No. Rex is too busy with his selfish life to be part of Sawyer's." She piled up the remaining crusts on her plate, leaving the chips untouched.

"How did you meet him?"

"Through mutual friends." Her lips pursed. "But I'm guessing what you're really asking is why I married him."

"Not necessarily." But at the same time… yeah. That was what he wanted to know. "Did you love him?" Evan's voice cracked on the *L* word. He'd never said *I love you* to any woman besides his mother. Not even to Addie when they'd been teens. She'd known though. At least he assumed she had.

"I think so." Addie's shoulders lifted. "I mean, I want to say yes, of course, but I'm not sure if I can. He was my escape. It sounds so horrible now, but I was a mess, Evan. My parents were so controlling." She paused at that, her obvious emotion rising like the tide, communicating more than words. "You know."

Yes, he did. They'd definitely forced a separation between Addie and himself. Evan understood why, but he wished they would have let the two of them at least remain friends. Except…he'd been so crazy about Addie at the time. What were the odds he would have been able to switch from love to like?

"I needed out, needed to break away from them," Addie continued. "And I naively thought he was my ticket." She met Evan's eyes, letting him glimpse the regret. "But he was the wrong ticket. I was so stupid to marry him. I think he cheated on me, but I never had any proof. And some people are so excellent at spinning things that you get all turned around and don't know which way is up." Sadness claimed her mouth. "Basically, he checked out not too long after we got married, and Sawyer was his excuse to get out."

Her stark, heavy pain brought to life something long dormant in Evan, like a match to a stack of brittle old newspapers.

He cared about her.

Cared that she had suffered. Cared that she had wounds. Simply cared.

And Evan hadn't allowed that to flicker in a long time. Sure, he cared about the trauma victims who fought to regain their lives on one of his trips, but they were more…safe. Addie was too…invasive. She didn't even have to try to get him to open up or let her in. Just being near her ripped wide the cavities he'd had on lockdown for years.

It was torture to see her drowning in the aftermath of her choices. And it was equally painful to know that Sawyer's dad wasn't involved in his life.

Evan had grown up that way for the most part. Dad had been around before his death, sure, but he'd been absent at the same time. Always more fond of drinking than his family. He and mom had fought once in a while. All verbal, at least. Evan was thankful for that. If his father would have laid a hand on their mother…just the thought made his vision turn red. But the spats had been plenty hard without that thrown in. Evan wasn't sure which was better—no father but a loving mother like Sawyer's situation, or a dad that had stuck around until his alcoholism had killed him in the form of a bar fight.

None of the above was the answer Evan wanted to give, and would, if he could have changed any of it. "I can't imagine not being there for my kid, not raising them. How does that happen? What kind of a person does that?"

Addie had taken a drink of water, and her eyes widened. She choked, hacking. She popped up and paced until the wheezing faded and her breathing went back to normal.

"You okay?" Evan got up and cleared their disposable plates, bringing them over to the trash can.

She nodded, taking another sip of water.

"Sorry if I upset you."

She cleared her throat. "I'm fine. I just…" Her head shook, and if he wasn't mistaken, new moisture shimmered.

What was going on? Had he offended her? "I'm not passing judgment on you, Addie. I just don't understand how your ex can do that to Sawyer. How he can be okay disappearing from his kid's life. I hate to see something like that affect a child like Sawyer. My dad made terrible choices, and Jace and I still have to live with them, even now. I just… I could never let that happen. I could never let a child of mine go through what I did as a kid."

* * *

*I could never let a child of mine go through what I did as a kid.* The air in Addie's lungs squeezed out at Evan's declaration. When he heard about Eli, would he think that's what their son had been through? Eli had a loving father though. The plan her parents had forced into existence had at least given their son that.

"But...don't you think that sometimes we're better for the trials we've been through? I'd like to think Sawyer will be. Even without his father involved. Somehow." She was reaching now, trying to ease the guilt, to repaint the story so she wasn't the villain.

"Sometimes yes. But if I could go back and make my dad committed and involved..." Evan swallowed. "I would do that in a heartbeat."

Evan had mentioned enough about his dad when they'd been in high school that Addie knew how much he'd struggled with their relationship. Or lack thereof.

"Do you wonder if you would have been better off without your father in your life? Like Sawyer?"

"It's hard to say. The best scenario would have been for our dad to be present and loving."

True.

"That's what is so hard to get over. Him not caring enough about us to make a change. I like to think that he loved us, but he sure didn't show it very well. Absentee fathers affect their kids for the rest of their lives, and I'm devastated that it's happening to Sawyer."

"Me too." Along with an ever-growing list of other things for Addie to regret.

"You know what happened with Luc Wilder, right?" Evan questioned, his features morphing to storm clouds. Evan was connected to the Wilder family now because his brother had married Mackenzie—Luc's twin. The Wilders had run a local guest ranch for generations and were well respected, well-known and well-liked. Addie secretly thought of them as Westbend royalty.

"Yes." Addie had heard the story when she'd moved to town. Luc's ex-girlfriend Cate had shown up at Wilder Ranch with a three-year-old daughter named Ruby, who he hadn't known existed. But the town had accepted Cate from the rumblings Addie had intercepted. Luc and Cate had even married and had twins last summer. Addie had silently cheered from the sidelines when she'd heard about their fresh start. It had given her hope that maybe her past could be redeemed from the ashes too.

"I realize I don't know all of the details of their situation, but when I heard…" Evan's head shook. "It shattered me for that little girl, spending the first years of her life without her dad. And for Luc, missing out on all of that. Who knows how that will affect him or her long term?" His expression morphed to thunder and lightning combined. "I have no idea how Luc forgave Cate for that. What a nightmare, abandoning your kid and not even knowing it. I can't imagine anything worse."

Any remnants of hope inside Addie plummeted to a swift death. Her stomach revolted and spun. How would she ever tell Evan about Eli now? He'd hate her—and according to what he'd just said, never forgive her. He'd likely never forgive himself, either, for not being present in Eli's life. Evan would see the situation as a repeat of his childhood, even though that choice had been taken from him. He would believe he'd abandoned their son.

So much for using the time spent with Evan to figure out how to tell him about Eli. So much for that new start void of potholes and mistakes she'd been gunning for in Westbend. At the rate she was going, Addie would need to move to a different country in order to outrun the black marks on her soul.

# Chapter Six

On Sunday morning, Evan was trapped between the pulpit and Bill Bronson, who was sitting two rows behind him and would no doubt like to continue their previous conversation about Old Westbend Weekend.

And in addition to that frustration it was Mother's Day.

Evan hadn't realized what day it was. Maybe he'd been working so hard that he hadn't noticed. Or maybe he'd been blocking out all of the Mother's Day stuff because he hadn't wanted to deal. Either way, the day had come as an absolute shock to his system. Especially when he'd sat down to find that the whole church service would be about mothers.

After the benediction, people stood, talking in their pews, a low rumble filling the sanctuary.

"Any chance you want to block for me with Bill Bronson?" Evan asked his brother.

Evan had sat with Jace and Mackenzie, plus the other two Wilder siblings and their spouses. During the service, Mackenzie had reached over and slipped her hand inside Jace's, then hadn't let go.

Evan could admit he'd experienced a moment of jealousy. It had passed quickly once he'd remembered who he was and the scars he carried. The ones his brother seemingly did not.

Jace quirked an eyebrow. "Now what kind of trouble are you in that you need to be avoiding the mayor?"

Evan released a heavy sigh. "He wants me to help out with Old Westbend Weekend."

Another questioning look from Jace.

"As the hometown hero. I guess Darian Nickert, who they'd had lined up, passed away."

"I'd heard that recently. That's too bad. And just what does this hero role have to do with you?"

Evan snorted. "My question exactly."

"I got you, brother." Jace slapped him on the back. They pooled into the aisle, and Mackenzie began talking to her brother and sister and their spouses.

"Bill!" Jace practically hollered the mayor's name.

Evan's jaw swung low. "You rotten scoundrel." He elbowed his brother in the gut, causing him to cover the spot and scoot a foot away. Didn't stop him from continuing to wave Bill Bronson in their direction though. "What did I ever do to you? Huh?"

"You roughed me up a couple of times when we were kids."

"We were playing. I couldn't help it that I was bigger and stronger than you."

Jace chuckled.

Evan groaned. "You know I hate to be in the limelight."

"That I do." If Jace's smile were any bigger it would break his face.

Evan should have known better than to ask his squirt of a little brother for help. Of course he'd take the opportunity to jab at Evan. That had always been their way. They were brothers. It only made sense. Evan had been off his game for too long, not seeing Jace on a regular basis. He was going to have to step it up.

"Bill, good to see you." Jace shook the man's hand. "I hear you'd like Evan to be part of Old Westbend Weekend." His brother was really throwing out the charm now, schmoozing, cinching the rope.

"Sure would. He's the perfect fit. The hometown hero gives out awards to a handful of kids who are honored as young heroes, and we need someone to fill that role who these kids can look up to."

Great. It was about kids. How was Evan going to say no now?

Despite what Bill believed, Evan *did not* fit the description of a hero. Not only had he taken years to pull himself out of the grips of his accident, but when he'd first begun leading groups, one of his trauma victims had a breakdown on the trail. He'd had to call in emergency services to rescue her. That's when he'd started partnering with Christopher. Before that he'd been too wild and careless, and someone had suffered greatly because of it. The woman was still a shell of her pretrauma self today. Evan knew because he checked up on her from time to time. He couldn't help feeling responsible for his part in what had happened.

See? Not a hero.

"Well, Bill, I'm happy to report that Evan was just telling me how much he'd like to help out." Jace's words snapped Evan back to the present. "He was saying what an honor it would be to take on that role."

But how could Evan step in when he'd soon be going to jail for beating his brother to a pulp?

"That's so great!" Bill boomed. He shook Evan's hand, which was limp, but the man pumped it numerous times anyway. "I really appreciate this, Evan. I truly do. You're going to be such an inspiration for those kids."

Hello, guilt.

"It's for the kids." Jace raised his eyebrows, challenging him.

"Jerk," Evan said for Jace's ears only, which earned a low chuckle of delight from his brother.

"There's a meeting this afternoon for the planning committee," Bill continued, oblivious to their heated undertones. "Would be great if you could be there. Two o'clock at the library."

Bill took off before Evan could make an excuse, tell him no, slug his brother.

Jace's palms went up, and he inched back from Evan. "I think there's a commandment about not murdering in church."

"Unfortunately for you, I was never very good at paying attention in church. I must have missed that one." He took a menacing step forward, and Jace morphed into his ten-year-old self, laughing, scooting to hide behind Mackenzie.

"Only wusses cower behind their wives."

"But she's tougher than I am!"

Mackenzie scrutinized the two of them, amusement evident. "Do you boys need a time-out?"

"No, ma'am." Evan flashed his most innocent of grins. "We were just talking about how Jace wants to help raise money to go toward scholarships for trauma victims who'd like to do an expedition but don't have the funds." In each group Evan took out, there was at least one scholarship for someone who couldn't afford the trip. At times he found grants or raised money for those spots. Sometimes he covered things out of his own pocket if nothing else came through.

"That's such a great idea, J!"

"That's exactly what we were talking about," Jace piped in, "and it is an excellent idea. I'm glad I thought of it. Maybe we can do a fundraiser in conjunction with Wilder Ranch."

Ugh. Jace had certainly turned that around to make himself look good. Evan rolled his eyes. Not that Mackenzie or Jace noticed. They were too enthralled with each other.

"I'll catch up to you in a bit." Evan left Jace and Mackenzie chatting with her family and took off down the aisle. He slipped out of the church and into the attached meeting room, finding a wall to lean against and hole up. What was he going to do now? How was he going to get out of the hero thing? He could tell Bill that he had social anxiety—which wasn't technically the truth. Or stage fright. Or…yeah, he was running out of excuses, but he'd pay a chunk of money to come up with one.

"Hi." Sawyer appeared and tugged on Evan's khaki athletic pants—which Evan could admit were a bit of a uniform with him. He'd thrown on a blue button-up shirt instead of a T-shirt, though, so he had to get some Jesus points for that.

"Hey, squirt."

"Up," the boy demanded, and Evan, not one to go against the flow, obeyed the order. Sawyer was getting more comfortable with Evan now that they'd spent some time together, and Evan found himself looking forward to seeing the kid.

He scanned for Addie's whereabouts.

There she was, on her tiptoes. "I'm guessing your mama's looking for you, little man."

Evan waved, and Addie came their way. She wore a flowered dress and a jean jacket, and she looked young and pretty and out of his league. Refreshed even. Evan would like to think his help at the B & B had something to do with that last thing.

"Sawyer make a run for it again?"

"You know it. I assumed he was at least safe at church, and that he was somewhere in this room, so I wasn't stressing too much." She spoke to Sawyer. "Though I would appreciate it if you figured out how to stick around, bug."

Evan and Sawyer were twins in that regard.

"Sawyer must have seen you from across the room and beelined for you."

Evan grinned at him. "That's nice. I like to see you too, kid."

"Bel?" So the beeline wasn't about him. It was about his dog. Figured.

"She's at home. They don't really like dogs in church."

Sawyer's brow wrinkled at that. Evan understood the sentiment. If it were up to him, Belay would go everywhere with him all of the time. She pretty much did. Except when he had to fly for trips. Then he had a neighbor who cared for Belay while he was out of town.

His attention returned to Addie.

"Happy Mother's Day." The soft smile on her face that had surfaced while watching Sawyer fell flat.

"Oh, um…thanks."

That had been a strange response. Except… the day might be hard for Addie because she didn't have a great relationship with her own mom.

"You okay?"

She went back to emotionless in an instant. "Yeah. It's just…that service." She winced, then wrapped her arms in a self-hug. "I imagine Mother's Day is hard for a lot of people."

Addie's voice gained momentum. "People like you, who've recently lost their mom. This is your first one without her. That has to be painful. I'm so sorry, Evan."

He swallowed a ball of memories and hurt. "Thanks. I can admit the day took me by surprise."

"Outside? I go outside now." Sawyer's request sounded good to Evan too. He'd be all right breaking out of here.

Were Addie's eyes glistening? She sniffled and didn't meet Evan's gaze. Was it just the day upsetting her? Or something more?

"I need to use the restroom, actually." Addie held open her arms for Sawyer, but his head shook with a vengeance.

"Outside." The cute little terrorist stated his demands more clearly this time, as if they hadn't caught them on the first round.

Evan laughed. "I'll take him out. Go ahead." His chin jutted toward the bathroom. Evan assumed Addie would refuse, but shockingly, she didn't.

"Okay, thanks." Head down, she scooted through people quickly, shoulders slumped like she was carrying the world on her back. Strange. Maybe Evan should follow and check on her. Or maybe his instincts were way off and she was fine. Everything Evan knew about women could fit neatly into the change compartment in his vehicle, so he stuck to the plan and took Sawyer outside.

Along the way, he earned a few speculative looks. But then, he was holding Addie's kid. And the town would certainly have known they dated in high school. Most everyone knew him because of his accident and amputation. It had rocked Westbend to the core. People had definitely rallied around his family after. Had brought meals or donated gas cards for the drive to the hospital. Something like that should have put a single mother under—but it hadn't, because Mom hadn't been alone. Dad might have been long gone, but the people of Westbend had risen to the challenge.

Maybe Evan did owe the town this hero thing. He let out a huff of frustration, and Sawyer imitated the sound.

"Exactly. You get me, squirt." Evan lowered the tyke to the ground, and they walked along the flower beds that were just beginning to bloom, stopping to check out an army of ants.

Evan wanted with everything in him to walk back inside that church and tell Bill Bronson in no uncertain terms that he wasn't a fit for the hero gig, that he couldn't do it, that he had the wrong guy.

But how could he do that when this town had given so much to his family? To his mom?

He already knew the answer—he couldn't.

So now instead of just helping Addie out, he was getting roped into helping the town. It all stank quite a bit like getting attached.

Even though that wasn't at all what he planned to do.

Addie camped out in a bathroom stall and used toilet paper to blot under her lashes. Her crying eyes were going to give her away the minute she escaped, she just knew it. But what could she do about it? She hadn't been expecting the service this morning to be all about Mother's Day…or for Evan to wish her a happy one.

That had been a blow. She felt like a heel. Like a scab that grew on a heel. Like the infection that grew on a scab on a heel.

Especially after their conversation last night.

Over the years, Addie had thought about a great many things regarding Eli and giving him up for adoption. About Evan and what that news would do to him.

But she'd never once put it together that she'd made Evan's worst nightmare come true. She'd effectively forced him to abandon a son he hadn't known existed.

How could she tell him the truth now?

It would kill him, which in turn would kill her. If Addie had thought revealing the truth about their son to Evan was going to be hard before, last night's declaration made it downright impossible.

The news she harbored would break Evan all over again. Addie had watched that unfold once. How could she be part of it happening a second time around?

She took five deep breaths and then forbade herself from any more tears. This definitely wasn't the right moment or place. Not when she was attending church for the first time in a long while. Ever, really. Addie hadn't been raised a Christian. She'd only decided to attend because she'd thought it would be good for Sawyer…and pathetically that it would seem beneficial for her to be seen at church as an upstanding member of the community. Good for business.

But this morning, it had been like Pastor Higgin had been speaking directly to her. Her heart had pounded, her skin had gone clammy. He'd talked about mothers. How the way a mother sacrificially and unconditionally loved her children mimicked how God loved his children.

But how could God love someone like her? Who'd done what she'd done? And now didn't know how to undo it?

Addie didn't have answers to any of that, and

she wasn't sure how to piece together and sort through all of her jumbled feelings, especially not with Mother's Day guilt heaped on top.

Satisfied that the tears had stopped leaking, she left the stall and went to the sink. She ran the warm water, letting it cascade over her fingers as the woman next to her swiped under her eyelashes and checked her reflection in the mirror.

When she caught Addie watching, she dropped her gaze.

"Mother's Day can be tough. I'm sorry if it is for you." Addie's offered comment was met with softening eyes and a flash of moisture.

"Ugh!" the woman exclaimed, hands jutting into the air as Addie turned off the faucet and used a paper towel. "I almost never cry. I'm usually not such an emotional person."

Addie's smile bloomed. "I've been extra emotional lately too."

"I'm Charlie."

"Addie. I'm somewhat new in town. I lived here for a few summers in high school, but that was ten years ago."

"It's good to meet another person who wasn't born and raised in Westbend." Charlie brightened, her light blue eyes contrasting so prettily with her red hair and creamy skin. "I haven't been here long. I own a mechanic shop. Charlie's Garage."

"That's so cool. I thought it was a guy who owned it."

Charlie laughed. "You're not the first."

"Did you want to talk about…" Addie didn't want to pry, but she felt the tug to ask, so she did.

"Nah, I'm okay now. Thanks. It's just… I'd like to be a mother, but that hasn't happened for me yet."

"That would be really hard, especially on a day like this. I'm sorry."

"Thanks." The two of them moved toward the exit together.

"So what do you do, Addie?"

"I'm reopening Little Red Hen Bed & Breakfast."

"How fun. We're both business owners."

"Except I have no idea what I'm doing." Addie's stomach churned at the admission.

"You should let me help you then." Charlie opened the door, holding it for her. "I owned another shop before I moved here but sold that one. I love to talk business. Anytime you have any questions, seriously, let me know." Charlie dug in her rounded purse that was made of license plates.

"That's so cute. Did you make it?"

"Me? Oh no. I'm not skilled in any kind of craft area." Charlie palmed her phone. "Give me your number and I'll send you a text. That way you have mine."

Addie rattled hers off. "Thank you so much. You have no idea what a relief it is to have you offer that. You're so kind."

Charlie's smile widened. "I'm also in need of friends. Who knows, we just might hit it off."

Addie thought they already had. After saying goodbye, she headed outside to find Sawyer and Evan. She'd been gone too long. Hopefully he wasn't annoyed or didn't have to be somewhere that she was keeping him from. And hopefully he assumed she'd been talking to people and not in the bathroom this whole time. Her lips twitched.

Addie found the two of them around the side of the small white church. They had sticks and were both drawing in the dirt. Her heart throbbed. *That could have been us with Eli.* Except it wouldn't have been. Not when she and Evan had both still been in high school. *You gave Eli the best life you could. Now stop thinking about it and him.*

That command was always hard on Mother's Day.

Evan spotted her and straightened.

She forced a smile, going for bright and not *just bawling in the bathroom stall.*

His forehead etched with creases. "Everything okay?" he asked.

So much for striving to be enough sunshine that he wouldn't notice she'd been upset. Addie kept playing the *all is well* card, infusing perkiness into her demeanor. "Yep. I just… I ran into someone inside. Sorry it took me so long."

"It's fine. We're good."

Sawyer hadn't even taken a second to acknowledge her presence. It was amazing how quickly he'd bonded with Evan. Usually he was more guarded around men, having grown up with just the two of them.

"You sure nothing is on your mind?" Evan asked. "I'm a pretty good listener."

Addie knew that from experience. "I just… I'm a horrible person."

He laughed. She didn't.

"How so?"

*Because I gave our son up for adoption without telling you.* Over the years, Addie had come to believe adoption had been the best choice for Eli. But if her parents would have allowed her to reach out to Evan, maybe he would have agreed, and then she wouldn't have had to live with this guilt and shame all of these years. They could have made the decision together.

Addie followed Sawyer, in step with Evan. "I shouldn't admit this, but I came to church today because I thought it would look good. That people would respect me and support me as a business owner if I did."

One of his shoulders scooted up. "Probably true."

"Embarrassing to confess though. But now that I'm here…it felt like Pastor Higgin was talking right to me. It was…awful."

Evan laughed again, and Addie's insides gave a painful squeeze of attraction.

"That happens a lot in church."

"What is that about?"

"God doing His thing. The Holy Spirit at work."

"I guess. It makes me kind of…uncomfortable."

"Me too sometimes. I think that's God's way of reminding us that maybe we have something to work on or that we need to trust Him about a particular situation."

Another bull's-eye. "Yeah. I guess. I'm new to all of this God stuff."

"That's okay." Evan offered his stick to Sawyer, who took it and went to town with one in each hand, dirt flying. He'd probably need two baths today. And his church clothes—a plaid button-up shirt and khaki shorts—would need the same. "God is good with newcomers. I was one too, at one point. We all were."

"When did you figure it all out?"

"I still haven't done that, but after my accident, after all of the anger, when I started hiking and climbing and getting out into nature—that's where I met God. He'd been right there all along, but the mountains, the sky, the stars, the rivers—it was like they were all shouting His existence. I couldn't ignore Him anymore." Evan's smile was wry. "Probably sounds crazy, right?"

"Actually, it makes perfect sense."

And maybe if nothing else in her life did, God would. Pastor Higgin had said there was nothing God couldn't love them through. That He was consistent.

Maybe Addie should try to find out if that was true, even for her.

# Chapter Seven

Addie kept monopolizing Evan's time. First at the B & B—though she could hardly blame herself for that. He was the one who'd insisted on helping her out. And now again at church. Surely he had better places to be than with her.

She'd seen his brother inside. And Jace's wife, Mackenzie, who was long and lean and ruggedly gorgeous to boot. The other Wilder siblings had been present too. While walking outside, Luc Wilder had held open the door for Addie. His wife, Cate, and their three girls had been with him, and Addie had been filled with so much longing for what they had—for the grace covering their past—that she had struggled to squeak out a thank-you.

At some point, Addie would work up the nerve to ask one of the Wilder siblings if they'd consider sending referrals her way for guests arriving before or needing to stay after their guest ranch experience. But she'd been too much of a mess to broach the subject today. She'd probably have burst into tears if one of them had said no.

"Do you need to go?" she asked Evan. "Sorry I kept you so long."

"I'm not in a rush. I might pop out to Wilder Ranch for lunch with Jace and Mackenzie. After that I have to…" Evan groaned.

"Run into a burning building? Perform brain surgery? Teach a sewing class?"

Humor momentarily flashed across his features. "Go to a meeting for Old Westbend Weekend."

What? So much for some Evan-free time to pull herself back together. "I'm going to that, but I didn't realize you were. The B & B is one of the sponsors for the weekend." Addie had used her entire limited advertising budget for the three-day event.

"I thought my brother might block for me today. Instead he totally kicked me under the bus as it roared by. He caught Bill's attention and volunteered me for the hero thing." The pure torment on Evan's face was almost comical. "I want to back out of it, but Bill played the 'it's for the kids' card, and now I think I'm trapped."

"What all does it entail?"

Evan's head quirked. "I'm not even sure. I've been so busy saying no that I don't have any details." His eyes widened. "You don't think there's any public speaking involved, do you? Because then I really am out."

Addie fought amusement. The adult version of Evan seemed so calm and collected. Like he could handle anything life threw at him. It was strangely reassuring to see him panic, to know she wasn't the only one drowning in the occasional bout of fear.

"I highly doubt there is. No way would Bill Bronson willingly give up an available microphone." After Bill had talked to Evan at The Fork and Spoon, he'd worked the crowd like he was still running for office.

"True. I'll have to ask some questions this afternoon."

"Look, Mommy!" Sawyer ran over to them. A grubby, slimy—and very dead—worm rested in the palm of his hand.

"Ew."

At her disgust, Sawyer showed the prize to Evan. "Good find. He looks like he's dead, though, so you'd better give him a proper burial."

"Yeah!" Sawyer hurried over to the patch of dirt. He plopped the worm onto the sidewalk and told it to "stay" just like he would Belay.

That made both of them laugh. Then he used one of the sticks as a shovel and began digging a hole.

"He's like a cat, always bringing me dead animals as gifts. I'm surprised he doesn't leave them for me on the doorstep."

Evan chuckled while waving toward the parking lot. She turned to see his brother and Mackenzie walking to their vehicle.

"Do you guys want to come out to Wilder Ranch for lunch? I'm sure they wouldn't mind two more. It's a happy sort of chaos there with all of the kids. Mackenzie's little sister Emma and her husband, Gage, have a son around Sawyer's age. The two of them could probably get into all kinds of trouble together."

Addie's heart constricted at the offer. No doubt Sawyer would love it. She wanted exactly what Evan was offering, but all of that was off-limits for her. She couldn't allow herself any more access into Evan's world or vice versa. Not with her still keeping their son under wraps. And ever since their conversation last night, Addie couldn't begin to imagine telling Evan about Eli.

Her original plans to come clean had been derailed indefinitely.

"We can't, but thanks. I've got to get Sawyer down for a nap." Addie wasn't about to attempt attending a meeting with a tired Sawyer, and she didn't have anywhere else in town for him to go.

Evan's face morphed from relaxed to taut, but he didn't press further. "Right. Okay. I guess I'll see you later then." After saying goodbye to Sawyer, he caught up with Jace and Mackenzie in the parking lot.

A momentary flash of loss ached in Addie's chest. A few days in Evan's presence and he was already showing her how different things could have been. It was like there was a life out there that she'd missed by taking the wrong path. It was shiny and warm and so, so out of reach.

And the worst of it was, until Evan, she hadn't realized just how much she was missing.

In the first three minutes of the meeting about Old Westbend Weekend, Bill Bronson launched into a history of the town, the event…and his childhood. What that last item had to do with anything, Evan couldn't imagine. But at least Addie had been right—Evan shouldn't have to do any public speaking. Bill had that down pat.

Not that Addie was present to confirm her theory. She had said she was coming, right? Maybe she was avoiding him. After that strange response at church to his lunch invitation, Evan wouldn't put it past her. She was so confusing…

one minute they were friendly, like they actually had a relationship and history between them. The next she was shutting him out.

Still, he shouldn't have invited them to Wilder Ranch today. It had been stupid on his part to put himself out there like that. To try to make things about more than him helping her with the B & B. Evan was assisting her in order to honor his mom, and he had better remember that.

Just because he and Addie were back in each other's lives momentarily didn't mean they were right for each other. Evan's job was never stationary. His apartment in Tennessee was almost always empty because he traveled so much. Attraction didn't equal rightness.

And then there was the fact that she and Sawyer deserved someone consistent. Someone who could love them fully without holding back. Someone who could let people in, who hadn't died emotionally a long time ago.

Evan definitely didn't fit that bill.

Between his dad's abandonment and his accident, Evan had lost a piece of himself. He lived adventure on a daily basis and risked it all, but he hadn't done the same with his heart since Addie. And did their relationship even count? They'd been too young for it to be real, hadn't they?

"We've got three days to showcase the history

of our city and prove we're still viable today, thus the Westbend—Then and Now theme of the weekend." Bill's chest puffed out as he strutted across the front of the room and spoke into a microphone. Overkill for a group of twenty. "And with all of these businesses represented and supporting, we're going to make a big push for tourism. As everyone knows, this is our biggest weekend. But why can't we have more? Old Westbend Weekend is just the start of what we can bring to this town."

A few people applauded, and Evan swallowed a groan. It was like Bill was giving a campaign speech even though he'd already been elected and in office for two years. The man could tone down the Westbend rah-rah a notch or two. But then again, that's why Bill was the mayor and Evan wasn't.

He maneuvered his prosthesis out of the way for a woman with red hair who was scooting by him to find herself a chair. And then Addie and Sawyer followed behind her.

Addie greeted Evan on the way by, but Sawyer had different plans. When he spotted Evan, he flashed the smile of all smiles and waved super big.

"Eban! Hi, Eban." His volume was way too high for the setting, which amused Evan to no end. He'd never been one for protocol. Addie turned and shushed Sawyer, panic written in every tight muscle, as Evan waved back at him.

The redhead took a seat one row behind, and Addie tried to follow. She pulled on Sawyer's hand, but the little rascal didn't budge. Addie huffed and dropped into the chair to Evan's right, probably just to get her rear into a seat and stop drawing attention to herself.

She motioned for Sawyer to come to her, but he shook his head. "No." Another too-loud word. More amusement surfaced in Evan.

Addie seethed, leaning closer. "Would you stop encouraging him?"

"What?" he whispered back. "What am I doing? I'm just sitting here. I can't help it if the little guy likes me more than you."

He'd meant it as teasing, but based on the angry heat billowing his direction, Addie hadn't taken it that way. She was definitely about to blow.

"Mommy, I don't be here." Sawyer's voice had dropped from the level ten he'd been operating at, but it was still enough to cause laughter from the people sitting closest.

Pink rushed Addie's cheeks, and sympathy flooded Evan. It was all fun and games to him because Sawyer's behavior didn't reflect back in his direction. Addie didn't have that luxury, and she was probably mortified even though she shouldn't be. Sawyer was just being a kid—a funny, entertaining one.

In an attempt to defuse, Evan opened his arms to Sawyer, who came right to him. The tyke was good for his ego. He tugged the stubborn guy up on his lap, and Sawyer sank back against Evan's chest like he was a safe place.

His heart gave a heavy thump that sounded oddly like a warning alarm.

While he might have plenty of reasons and determination not to fall for Addie all over again, Evan was way too close to the edge of that cliff when it came to her kid.

After texting with Charlie this afternoon and realizing that both of their businesses were sponsoring Old Westbend Weekend, Addie had hoped to sit with the woman. They'd met in the parking lot and walked in together, but that was as far as they'd gotten. Sawyer had thwarted that plan with his cheeky, stubborn *embarrassing* display.

Addie was thankful Evan had curbed things before they'd escalated by scooping Sawyer onto his lap. She was also reeling from the two-year-old's betrayal.

Of course Sawyer wasn't being malicious. Her son didn't realize that his newfound infatuation with Evan was painful for her on so many levels.

Sawyer only recognized that Evan was fun and paid attention to him. These were big things in the toddler world.

They would be big things in Addie's world too if she let them, but that wasn't an option.

Alma Dinnerson raised her hand. "I'd like to bring up an issue."

Bill Bronson forked over the microphone. Alma looked at the mic like it was foreign to her, then proceeded to yell into it, oblivious to the rumble of amusement rippling through the room. "I'd like to get a permit to sell food from my food truck. I live so close to Main Street, I feel like I'll be able to make some money during Old Westbend Weekend."

She tapped the microphone and handed it back to Bill, who spoke without using it. "That doesn't really have anything to do with Old Westbend Weekend planning."

"Why not?" Alma cranked out.

"Because it doesn't. If you want a permit to sell food outside your home, you'll have to go to a city council meeting."

Alma's gaze swooped from one side of the room to the other. "Well, what kind of meeting am I at?"

Addie smothered a snort and met Evan's eyes.

His were crinkled and unguarded—the opposite of what they'd been when he'd escaped from her at church earlier.

A shiver cascaded down her spine.

"You're at the meeting about Old Westbend Weekend." Bill said.

"And that's exactly when I want to have my food truck!" Alma threw her hands up in confusion.

Bill leaned closer to Alma, and everyone strained to hear. "Are you talking about that cart you have for hot dogs and pretzels and such?"

"Yes."

"That's not really a food truck."

"It is. That's what the kids are calling them these days."

Bill sighed.

Addie—and pretty much everyone else—could no longer hide their laughter. Still, Alma was undeterred. Bill finally told Alma they'd discuss her needs later and then went back to explaining his agenda. Evan should be reassured that the man wouldn't be giving up time in front of the crowd during Old Westbend Weekend.

Sawyer scooted off Evan's lap and down to the floor. Addie tensed, worried he might make a break for it, but then he just plopped down on his behind and began messing with Evan's shoelaces.

Addie handed him a small car, and he drove it around and over Evan's shoe like it was a mountain to be conquered. Evan gave Sawyer a thumbs-up and a grin. How was he so comfortable with Sawyer? It hurt to see them bonding. So much. Had she been wrong to come back to Westbend after all this time? If she'd stayed away, she wouldn't be watching the father of her first son entertain her second son.

Sawyer grabbed Evan's leg—only it was the one with the prosthesis.

Addie leaned closer. "Are you sure he should be doing that? I can tell him to stop."

Her whisper was met with a quick shake of Evan's head and a cramped brow. "He's fine."

Sawyer touched the leg again, his curiosity growing. Maybe he could tell that it wasn't flesh and bones. Who knew exactly what was going through his little mind? And then, horror of all horrors, he sprawled on the ground and looked straight up Evan's pant leg.

Addie's mouth fell open. Oh no. She swallowed a moan of humiliation for the second time in a matter of minutes and the urge to rip her son off the floor. Evan wasn't overreacting, so why should she? Still, every pore on her body began a synchronized sweat. She removed her jean jacket, stuffing it partway into her bag so that she could still scoop up Sawyer and tear out of the room at any moment.

All she wanted to do was prevent this situation from spiraling out of control the way she envisioned.

If Evan could read her mind right now, he'd be rolling his eyes. And then he looked at her and did exactly that. As if to say, *Calm down, Addie. I've got this. I'm not uncomfortable with me. Why do you have to be?*

Instead of shying away or covering anything up, Evan raised his pant leg. Sawyer inspected the metal that connected to the base that filled Evan's tennis shoe. He squeezed it. He peered inside the shoe.

*Pease don't say anything out loud. Pease.*

Two-year-olds—Sawyer in particular—weren't exactly known for their filtering abilities.

Just as quickly as Sawyer's interest spiked, it faded. He popped up from the floor and came over to her. "Snack?"

Relieved, Addie rummaged through the bag until she found an item he approved of. Goldfish. Instead of crawling into her lap to eat them, he went back to Evan.

*Ouch, kid. After I birthed you and raised you on my own. A little loyalty would be nice.*

So would a father for Sawyer.

She winced. Addie had always avoided that

thought. Always hoped that Sawyer was better off with just her since she was consistent. But now that she'd begun to see him with Evan… the idea was taking shape, growing, acting like it had a chance of ever happening.

*Well, it doesn't. Certainly not with Evan.* Not with their past and all that he didn't know. And once she did figure out a way to tell him about Eli, he'd never forgive her. He'd confirmed last night how devastating that scenario would be.

Addie's breathing evened out as Sawyer ate his snack and didn't show any more interest in Evan's prosthesis. She would have thought she would know better than to get uncomfortable about something like that, but she'd done the whole mom-freak-out, what-is-my-kid-going-to-say-or-do-wrong panic. Unnecessarily so. Evan had handled the whole thing with ease.

Addie had always known her parents had been wrong to keep the truth about Eli from Evan. Seeing the man Evan had turned out to be only confirmed that.

If she could press Rewind and go back in time, she'd do it all differently, even though she didn't know what that altered path would look like. She'd been stuck then, and she was stuck now.

Coming to Westbend was supposed to be Addie's restart and redo, but it was turning into a repeat.

## Chapter Eight

Bright and early on Monday morning, Addie and Sawyer were buckled into her small SUV, heading to meet with Charlie before her garage opened. After the Old Westbend Weekend meeting yesterday, Charlie had asked Addie if she could make the next morning work. And since Addie was desperate for help with the B & B and up at first light with Sawyer anyway, she'd jumped on the opportunity.

She'd spent Sunday afternoon knocking out a couple projects on her list while Evan had done the same at his mom's, though he'd offered to work with her at the B & B again today.

Addie turned into the parking lot for the garage, which was located on the side of the building. The Charlie's Garage sign was made to look vintage, though Addie doubted it was. The building, on the other hand, had been around awhile. Two large glass roll-up doors flanked the front. Windows to what must be Charlie's apartment were located on a second level.

Addie released Sawyer from his car seat and stepped around to the front of the building even though Charlie had said to meet her around back. A peek through the glass-paneled door revealed a bright, clean and airy space. Organized tools and parts hung on the walls and filled shelves. Since Addie was so inept with vehicles, any time she'd needed a mechanic it had been akin to having a root canal. To think that she could go to Charlie for oil changes or repairs was a complete relief.

Sawyer had scooted down the front of the building. "Come on, buggy-bear. Let's go."

He ran back her way. "I bugaboo, Mommy."

"Bug-a-bean?"

His head shook, and he crossed his arms with a huff of frustration. Comical on a two-year-old.

"Okay." She stretched out the word. "But bugaboos get caught and squished."

Sawyer screeched with delight and managed two steps before Addie captured him. She pretended to squash him until he giggled. Pretty much the best sound in the world.

"I'm doing all of this for you, you know." She was referring to the bed-and-breakfast, of course, but Sawyer didn't know that.

"Okay, Mommy. Do it again." She laughed.

She plunked Sawyer back on the ground, held his hand and they rounded the building together. Hopefully her little bundle of energy would be willing to entertain himself with the activities she'd tossed into her ever-present bag so that she'd be able to glean wisdom from Charlie. Sawyer had survived yesterday's Old Westbend Weekend meeting, but she was asking a lot of him during this stage in their lives.

At the back of the garage, stairs led up to an apartment. At the bottom, there was a patch of grass and a patio filled with a table, umbrella and chairs plus a small sandbox with toys.

Charlie was sitting at the table, a mug perched in front of her with her nose in what looked to be a devotional. It was unusually warm for spring, so they'd planned to take advantage, though Addie had packed an extra layer for her and Sawyer in case the morning chill was too much.

"Good morning," Addie called out.

"Hey, guys." Charlie stood and gave Addie a hug.

Once Sawyer spotted the sandbox, he tried to pull away from Addie's grip. *Oh no you don't, mister.* Addie had endured enough of his escapes and antics lately. She was holding on.

Charlie's head quirked. "You can let him play

in the sandbox. I have it here for the parents with kids waiting to get their cars serviced. I promise it's okay."

Addie's shoulders crashed down, and she freed Sawyer. He flew over to the toys and happily settled on the edge of the sandbox. "Sorry. I'm a little uptight lately with all that's going on with the B & B. And Sawyer's been quite the busy boy, always running ahead or escaping." Or looking up Evan's pant leg.

"No problem. I totally get that. Starting a business is a lot of work and stress." Charlie resumed her seat.

Addie dropped her oversize bag onto the ground and took the chair to Charlie's right. "So you're telling me I'm not crazy? Because I'm beginning to feel that way sometimes."

"I'm a car doctor, and I am officially diagnosing you as not crazy."

Addie grinned. "I will accept that diagnosis. Thank you."

"There's coffee if you want." Charlie motioned to the tray that held a carafe, cream and sugar.

"I do want." Addie took the extra mug. "Thank you for this. And for meeting with me. And for letting Sawyer be a kid."

Part of her stress always came from people who expected kids to sit still and be quiet, who believed they should be seen and not heard. Completely unrealistic in Addie's opinion. Yes, she wanted Sawyer to behave and be kind, but he'd never been the type to draw quietly or stay in one place for too long.

Addie should have known that Charlie would be different with Sawyer. Especially with how much she wanted children. Addie sympathized with that craving Charlie had. Sawyer was the best thing that had ever happened to her.

"So, you said you owned a garage before this one?"

"I did, but I sold it. I had to go outside of a certain radius to start a new one, and my brother Finn used to live here and work at Wilder Ranch. Do you know the Wilders?"

"Who doesn't? They're like Westbend royalty."

"Ha! Right. Well, Finn's planning to buy a ranch—once he finds the right one for sale—and move back here, and I thought it would be nice to live by family. So that's how I ended up in Westbend. Hopefully I'll like small-town living, and if not, I could always sell or move again. Though I'd really prefer not to."

"And how's business?"

"Good. Growing slowly, but that's normal." Charlie took a sip of coffee and leaned against the back of her chair, broadcasting relaxation.

"But we're not here to talk about me. We're here to talk business. And if you happen to fill me in on the guy you were deep in conversation with outside after church, I would also consider that official business."

Addie laughed but it turned into a groan.

"Never mind." Charlie put her palms up. "You don't have to—"

"You're helping me out. I can give you some of the dirt." Addie swallowed. "Evan Hawke. I knew him—dated him—when I was a teenager. We met when I lived here one summer in high school." *And now I'm trapped in a terrible world where I want to be near him but shouldn't. Need to tell him something that will break him, but I don't know how.*

Charlie winced. "High school was not a good time for me. I can't imagine running into anyone I had a crush on back then. And it would be a crush, because no one asked me out."

"What? How is that possible? You're so amazing and put-together."

Her lips tucked up at the corners. "Aw, thanks. But I'd definitely rather not relive that time."

"I hear that. I was always the oddball at school, showing up with rice and adobo or rice and *sinigang* in my lunch. Rice and anything. Eventually I started packing pizza and macaroni and cheese just so I'd stop sticking out. It

took me a while to be comfortable with myself."
Age had helped. So had a certain teenage boy
seeing her and appreciating her for exactly who
she was. Now Addie would pack whatever she
wanted for lunch and not care what anyone else
thought. "I didn't expect to see Evan in town.
It's definitely thrown me for a loop, process-
ing…all of that. He's been helping me on the B
& B, pitching in without getting paid because
he said he wants to honor his mom, who was
basically a single mother."

"Wow. That's seriously generous."

"Isn't it?" After seeing how amazing Evan
was with Sawyer during the meeting yesterday,
hope had begun to sprout that maybe Addie
*could* tell him about Eli and that he'd handle it
with the ease he did everything else. But what
about his issues with his dad? Hurts like that
didn't just fade away. They stayed with a person,
suffocating and making themselves known. Just
like Evan's comments about not understanding how Luc could forgive Cate—and what a
nightmare it would be to abandon a child—had
haunted her since he'd said it.

Sawyer brought a bucket of sand over to
show Addie, then returned to dump it into the
sandbox. A glint of longing flashed as Charlie
watched him play.

*God, can you drop a baby in this woman's*

*lap? She'd be an amazing mother. I can already tell.* Since church yesterday, Addie had been talking to God in a constant stream. Pastor Higgin had said to go to Him with anything, so that's what she'd been practicing. With each prayer, she was becoming more relaxed, more comfortable—like she was chatting with a friend. Except when Evan came to mind. Then her prayers turned to begging—*God, show me what to do. Help me know how to fix this.* Her biggest fear was that the situation wasn't fixable.

"Hello? Are you open?" A man dressed in a fishing vest and carpenter khakis stepped around the back of the building. Pete Deller. Addie recognized him as a town staple, and the best fly-fishing guide around. He was also rumored to smell like fish no matter what he did to alleviate the stench. Addie had never gotten close enough to test the theory.

"Not yet," Charlie answered. "I open in about thirty minutes, but you can leave your keys in the drop box."

"When does Charlie get in? I don't need a woman fixing my car, messing things up."

Addie swallowed a gasp.

"'Bout thirty minutes," Charlie answered. "What's wrong with it, so I can let Charlie know?"

"It's making a weird noise." Pete cleared his

throat for at least ten seconds before Addie realized he was imitating the car's strange sound.

She watched Sawyer in the sandbox to hide her amusement.

"I'll relay the message." Humor threaded Charlie's response. "Just put your key in an envelope, write your contact info on it and leave it in the drop box, okay, sir? There's a pen hanging there for you to use."

Grumbling accompanied Pete's shuffle back toward the parking lot, and a strong fish smell wafted their way. Addie slipped her knuckles under her nose to block it. How was that possible? Did it live under his fingernails? Did he carry around fish in his pocket?

Addie waited for Pete to round the corner before commenting. "So that really is a thing."

"What is?" Charlie asked.

"The fish smell."

"He's *known* for that?"

"Yeah. I always thought it was an old wives' tale."

"This town can be a little quirky sometimes."

"You're telling me." Addie motioned to where Pete had just disappeared around the corner. "How do you just let that fly?"

"The smell?"

Addie laughed. "No. The attitude. Doesn't it

offend you when someone talks that way about you fixing a car?"

"Oh. Lots of women come here because I'm female. Some men don't care either way. Occasionally one stumbles in and asks for Charlie assuming the owner is a guy." She shrugged. "Sometimes I let them think what they want, fix their car, and send them on their way. Sometimes I clue them in."

"I want to be you when I grow up. I care way too much what people think. Especially when it comes to the B & B. I feel like public opinion is going to dictate its success."

"It will in a way. You need happy customers and referrals, yes. But you're also not going to be able to please everyone. It's impossible. There are a lot of hard people in the world. I just try to focus on the humor instead of bitterness."

"That's a good plan. I'm impressed."

"Don't be." Charlie flashed a bright white grin. "You just happened to catch me on a good day."

Evan reattached the painted cupboard doors to the cabinets, the zzz-zzz of the drill filling the strangely silent B & B. Addie and Sawyer were due back soon. She'd had a meeting this morning, but he'd had time, so he'd used the key she'd left him under the mat and let himself in.

Three left to go and then he'd text her to see what project she wanted to start on next.

At the Old Westbend meeting yesterday, Evan had found out that the hometown-hero role required only that he stand on stage, let them say something about him—gag—and then hand out awards to the kids. That part he was fine with. They were honoring some pretty cool kids at the festival, including one with physical limitations like him.

A car engine rumbled, and Evan paused to listen through the front window. Belay jumped up, tail wagging in anticipation, mouth lifted in that doggie grin.

"What is it, girl? Do you hear your boy?"

Evan moved on to the next cupboard door as Belay gave a woof of approval, her whole body wriggling with excitement. Seconds later, Sawyer burst inside. He greeted Belay with a hug, and the two of them spun in circles.

Addie didn't follow. Evan finished the last door, left the drill on the countertop and peeked out front. She was wrestling something out of her vehicle on the passenger side.

"Need some help?" He arrived in time to see her give the machine a final yank. The floor sander broke free and almost toppled her over. "Or you can do it yourself."

She laughed. "There's another in the back for

edging. I was determined to bring both home in one trip."

Evan opened the rear door. "And I see your stubbornness has paid off."

"Yep." She beamed, leaning on the sander. "I couldn't fit this guy in the back, so I laid the front seat all the way down and managed to wedge it in. I've become proficient at getting things to fit in this vehicle that don't want to comply."

"I bow to your cramming skills." He removed the edger from the back and closed the door.

Wherever Addie had been this morning, she'd dressed in jeans and sandals along with an avocado-colored shirt. Evan swallowed. Those gorgeous eyes of hers popped even more than normal today. One look and she could ask him for pretty much anything and get it. *Except for your jaded heart.* True. Evan wouldn't be gifting that monstrosity to anyone he cared about.

Yesterday evening he'd received a text message from the woman he'd dated two years ago. You really did a number on me, Evan Hawke. For the longest time, I couldn't figure out what was wrong with me or why you ended things as abruptly as you did. Evan hadn't given her much for answers at the time, because he hadn't had them. *I just can't* had been the response running through his head. And when she'd pushed for details, he'd scrammed and stopped responding to her. Not his proudest moment.

Her text yesterday had gone on to say that she was getting married and finally knew what real love looked like. Evan had hung his head long after receiving it, trying to decide if he should respond and what to say if yes. Eventually he'd sent a text saying he was sorry for the hurt he'd caused and that he was happy for her. There had been nothing wrong with his ex-girlfriend, and Evan hated that she'd trudged through that pain because of his issues.

That had been the end of their communication, but it had been a blatant reminder for Evan to keep his distance from any romantic feelings regarding Addie. She deserved more than his brokenness. And so did Sawyer. If Evan were to get involved with her and then panic, all three of them would suffer.

"So I take it we're doing some sanding today?"

"Yep!"

"I've never known anyone to be so excited about sanding wood floors."

She laughed. "I just had such an encouraging meeting with Charlie this morning. It put me in a good mood."

"Charlie?"

"Yeah. Charlie Brightwood. She owns the garage in town. I met her at church when you took Sawyer outside for me."

"Got it." Charlie was a she. Evan was happier than he should be about that news.

They lugged both of the machines inside.

"I'm going to change. Be right back." Addie scurried off to the back bedroom and returned a minute later with her hair piled on top of her head and her work clothes on—cutoffs and an old T-shirt that looked like it had been around awhile. Still, she was jaw-dropping. The kind of pretty that sank into your bones and demanded to be appreciated.

"Evan." Addie turned in a slow circle in the kitchen. "This is amazing! It looks fantastic."

Her response…yeah. It might be why he was here. If he could roll his eyes at himself, he would. Helping Addie had started because he'd wanted to do something his mom would have loved and appreciated, but Evan was afraid it was becoming about more.

Stupid on his part.

After Old Westbend Weekend, he'd go back to his career and Addie would open the B & B. They'd probably never see each other again. Plus, yesterday's text and his track record spoke for itself. Evan had no desire to glance in his rearview mirror and see another woman he'd run from left in the dust. Especially one with a kid. Abandoning an innocent child, even in a dating relationship, would kill him. And he didn't trust himself to stay.

An ache erupted in his chest, causing him to rub a hand over the wound. What was it about Addie that held him captive? How could a relationship from the past still have such a hold on him? As a teen, he'd fallen for Addie, the girl—her laugh, her humor, her gigantic heart. But Addie as an adult was so much more. Same heart, only bigger. So much drive, so determined to reopen the B & B, honor Alice and Benji, create a legacy for Sawyer. Plus, she was a *really* great mom—loving and patient and playful. She'd been a really good friend, too, once upon a time. Evan missed that. He missed what they'd had before their actions had caused things to spiral out of control, before her parents had separated them. Could they ever have that friendship back? And was he wrong to wish for it?

*Yes, you're wrong to wish for it, because it would never stop at friendship, and you know it. How many times do you have to be reminded you have half a heart? That you've never seen a relationship done right? You can't do that to Addie or Sawyer. They need better than you.*

"I. Love. This. Kitchen." Addie broke into a happy dance that was equal parts adorable and terrible. Her arms were going everywhere, her body resembling a convulsion.

"I had no idea you were such a terrible dancer."

She laughed. "Come on, Evan! A happy dance has no rules."

"My leg prevents me from dancing."

"Excuses!" She raised a finger like a feisty little pirate might when they wanted someone to walk the plank. "If you can climb a mountain, you can dance."

"Probably true, but I don't really have any desire to find out."

Her chest fluttered up and down as she caught her breath, eyes sparkling. "Wuss." She spun around the kitchen, arms out. "With everything done in here, I can check this space off the list. I don't know why I jumped to another project before putting the cupboard doors back on. Thank you, thank you, thank you." She leaped across the kitchen and threw her arms around his neck, landing against him with an *oomph*, all soft and warm and tempting.

It took Evan's brain a second to wake up, to realize what was happening. He tightened his arms around her, inhaling Addie. She smelled like strawberries and sunshine and happiness.

She let go without even a hint of discomfort, leaving Evan floundering. Finally, he spoke.

"You're welcome. Of course. It's just cupboard doors."

"It's so much more, and you know it."

Was she referring to his work at the B & B? Because he wasn't. And yes, he did know it.

## Chapter Nine

Addie surveyed the living room with her hands on her hips. "Furniture first." They'd have to get it all moved into the kitchen—on the tile—in order to attack the wood floors.

"Yes, ma'am," Evan quipped.

She grimaced. "I was being bossy, wasn't I? Sorry about that."

"No more than usual."

She threw a pillow at him, beaning him on the back. He laughed and maneuvered a chair from the living room into the kitchen. "So what all did you and Charlie discuss? She's sure getting a lot of credit for an hour meeting." He raised his eyebrows as if to say, *And what am I getting for all of my help?*

*A hug that shouldn't have happened.* One would think with all of the turmoil churning inside her over Evan, Addie could keep to herself. And yet she'd just thrown herself at him like he was hers for the taking when nothing could be further from the truth.

Addie pushed against the sofa and it didn't budge, so Evan joined her. They slid it into the space in the kitchen between the island/countertops and the breakfast nook.

"She helped me out with a bunch of stuff for the business. Some numbers, some marketing."

They moved back into the living room. "That's great." He carried a chair into the kitchen, and she did the same with a side table.

"I'm just so relieved to have her advice on some things. It takes the pressure off trying to research and figure it out for myself."

"I can tell. I'm glad."

Addie bent to roll up the living room rug. "Oh! Charlie also suggested I start Instagram and Facebook pages for the B & B. That way people can tag it if they're staying here and I can post pictures. It's free advertising, basically."

"Smart."

The two of them both lifted an end of the rug. When Evan straightened, he winced as if he'd twisted something.

"You okay?"

"Yep. Fine." He moved slowly, carefully as they set the rug up on its end against the kitchen cabinets.

"I looked up your business page. You have some really great photos on your Instagram. Do you hire a professional?"

"No. I enjoy fiddling around myself, catching a good shot."

"Really? That's impressive. I'm not great with a camera except for the odd moment that I actually remember to capture whatever Sawyer is doing. I don't suppose..."

"What?"

"I was just going to say that I don't have a good camera, and maybe, if you don't mind, and if you're still around, I was wondering if you'd help me take some photos of the finished B & B for the website and social media."

"Definitely. I'll still be in town. Especially since I got roped into the hometown-hero thing."

Addie couldn't be happier about that. The man was built for the role.

"What's that smile for?"

"I just... I'm kind of glad you got roped into it. I think you're a perfect fit."

His head shook. "I'm nowhere near a hero. I've made plenty of mistakes over the years."

"Oh, yeah? Like what?" *You certainly won't be able to top mine.*

Evan told her about the woman who'd had a breakdown. "And there were other failures too. One guy broke his ankle on one of the expeditions. And another ran out of his medication. I should have known to check for things like that and been prepared. But I learned all of that along the way."

What had Addie learned along the way? She'd made plenty of mistakes, but the difference between her and Evan was that he'd fixed his. Addie's weren't fixable. Telling Evan about Eli wasn't going to make everything better. For him, it would only make things worse. It might bring relief from her guilt, but it would create his worst nightmare.

How could she do that to him?

Except…hadn't she just questioned if he *could* handle the news about Eli after how great he'd been with Sawyer at the Old Westbend meeting? "Evan…"

"Yeah?"

"At church yesterday, did you see Luc and Cate Wilder together with their girls?" Addie's heart had swelled in size at the picture of redemption they'd made.

His brow furrowed, and he nodded.

"You mentioned how you would struggle in Luc's shoes, with how Cate didn't tell him about Ruby right away, but…" Her words chased each other in circles as she scrounged for the right ones. "Wouldn't you say that something amazing came from the mess of their past?"

*Please. Give me an opening. Give me some hope.*

A shrug answered. "Their story is redemptive, that's for sure. Maybe it wasn't as hard for Luc to work through what happened because he had a good father growing up. A consistent, present one. Maybe that gave him the grace to forgive Cate, to overcome something that would take down a lesser man. Like me."

*But you're not a lesser man.* If only her believing that could change how his father's actions had affected him. But Evan's wounds ran deep. And the information she held would break him open like a canyon. The organ inside Addie's chest cracked in two. She swallowed to combat the dry sand filling her throat, anything she'd hoped to say about Eli fleeing, then peeked out the front window, buying time to lasso her wavering emotions.

She'd left the front door propped open, and Sawyer and Belay were sticking to their usual pattern—and their allowed area on the porch. Addie would love to let Sawyer go a little farther out and play in the yard, but it wasn't fenced, and she didn't trust him not to escape.

Sawyer threw a ball that Evan must have brought along, and Belay took off after it, her collar jingling. She brought it back to Sawyer and dropped it at his feet, that perma-smile in place.

When Addie turned back to the living room, Evan was sitting in the remaining chair with his prosthesis detached. He'd worn shorts today, making it easily accessible.

"We wrecked you moving furniture, didn't we?"

His lips curved, but his concentration stayed on the leg. "No. I'm just making an adjustment. It keeps pinching." Looked like he was adding a layer of sock to the end of his stump.

Sawyer tore into the house. "Eban, Eban." He ran right up to the man and leaped into his lap. The prosthesis flew out of Evan's grip, skittering across the floor.

Silence. And then Evan burst out laughing.

Sawyer joined him, though he probably didn't have a clue what the joke was about. He pointed at the prosthesis lying in the middle of the floor. "Leg."

"Yep." Another wheeze of laughter came from Evan. "You're right, squirt. Any chance you'd be willing to grab that for me?"

Far more undaunted than any adult would be, Sawyer hopped down and retrieved the limb for Evan.

"Watch this." Evan reattached the prosthesis, and it made a funny sound. Like someone passing gas. Sawyer giggled hysterically. "Trapped air needs to get out of the socket when I put the leg on."

Sawyer didn't care for any of the details, just the funny sound. "Again, again." He clapped.

Evan did an encore to rave reviews from the two-year-old. Once Sawyer realized the show was over, he ran back outside, presumably to find Belay.

"Did I turn you off there with the leg fart?" A hint of vulnerability threaded Evan's question.

"Leg fart?" Addie laughed. "No." If anything he'd done the opposite. He was so comfortable with himself, with his prosthesis, with Sawyer. It only upped what she felt simmering under the surface.

"When I need an adjustment, this thing can make the worst noises at the worst times." Evan chuckled again. "Thankfully I don't have an office job. That would be an interesting explanation. Although one time I was in church." He cringed. "Mortifying."

"I can't even imagine. You handle it so well though. I'd want to crawl through the cracks in the floor."

"I was that way at first. Everyone stares at you when you have a prosthesis. I finally realized they weren't gawking at me, just the leg.

It's usually curiosity, nothing malicious. I've gotten used to it."

Which only made him more appealing. *Focus on the B & B, Addie Ricci. Not the man you're keeping secrets from.*

Sawyer and Belay ran inside the house and up the stairs.

"Sawyer Kane." She included his middle name so that he'd know she meant business. "Don't go in the Monarch Room. That's the one with the door shut." Addie didn't want him messing up what she'd already done. He didn't respond, so she walked to the base of the stairs.

"Did you hear me, mister?"

"We hearded you, Mommy!" he called down. Cute that he was including the dog in his answer. Belay was probably the better behaved out of the two of them.

She joined Evan back in the living room. "That kid. He used to be such a mama's boy. When he was little, he'd sit in my lap and let me read to him. He'd always stop by for a snuggle in the midst of playing. But now that he's getting older, it's like he doesn't need me anymore."

"He's two. Didn't you just change his diaper a little bit ago?"

"Touché."

Evan stood and walked to the far side of the room, studying the floors. There were a few dark spots near the wall that separated the living from the dining room. "Are you sure we should be taking this on? This seems like a big project."

"I don't really have a choice. But you don't have to help. Seriously, Evan. I can—"

"Stop." Evan went to inspect the sander and edger. Addie wasn't sure which one would be easier for him to use with his leg. The belt sander was humongous, but the edging sander might be harder for him if he had to bend over or put too much pressure on his prosthesis.

Again, she'd let him figure it out. Evan was a big boy. He didn't need her hovering.

Something flew in the open front door, and Addie screeched and ducked, arms landing protectively over her head. Whatever it was, there were more than one.

"What in the world?"

"Birds," Evan responded. "They took off for the dining room."

They followed. Addie gripped the back of Evan's T-shirt, using him as a shield.

"Really?" He glanced over his shoulder, amusement lighting his eyes.

"What?"

He chuckled. When he stepped into the dining room, the birds went wild, swooping from side to side, squawking and complaining. One dove at the other, coming within a foot of Evan.

"They're fighting each other." He jumped back into Addie, and the two of them retreated to the doorway.

She stayed behind him. Birds outside in a birdbath, at a feeder or perched in a tree were all good things. Birds waging war in her dining room? Not so much. And speaking of the dining room, when they got the birds out, they needed to move the furniture from there too. The wood floor stretched through the space, though thankfully it wasn't as worn or abused. They also had a china cabinet left from Tita to figure out how to maneuver. The sale of the house had included any furniture, and Addie had burst into happy, nostalgic tears when she'd found the piece still in great shape.

She peeked around Evan as the birds' squawks became more agitated. They were flying right for the dining room entrance. She saw them first, but Evan was busy glancing back at her. "I'll protect you." He winked.

Addie ducked.

Evan looked back to the dining room, let out a yelp and dove down.

Addie laughed so hard she wheezed. "I'm so glad you were here for me."

The birds were back in the living room—with the open door only yards away—but both continued to swoop and fly around in confusion and agitation.

"What do you mean? I had your back." When one bird dipped again, Evan ducked behind Addie, using her as a shield like she'd just been doing to him.

"More like I have yours." Laughter bubbled again. "Oh my. I really have to use the bathroom. That's what having babies does to you. Stop hiding back there! You're supposed to be protecting me!"

Evan stood straight again, his head slanted, questions brimming.

She'd said babies. *Oh no, oh no, oh no.* "A baby," she clarified. What had she done? This wasn't the time or place to drop news like that on the man.

*Though you do need to. Even if it wounds him beyond repair. You can't let him walk back out of your life next week without knowing.* Her laughter died. She didn't even argue with herself. It was true. She couldn't.

"I'll get you to the bathroom. Come on." Evan tugged her behind him, holding on to her hand as he did. Even that small gesture made every part of her ache with longing and remorse.

*You can't have him, Addie. All you can do now is pray he survives the revelation.*

\* \* \*

Evan scooted sideways, watching the birds as he did. They'd both perched on a curtain rod, frozen like a kid pretending to play hide-and-seek even though they were in plain sight.

He'd grabbed Addie's hand and pulled her close behind him in order to aid her escape—and get her to the bathroom—but now he just wanted to pause like the bird so that she'd stay pressed against his back. Her breath was shallow and punctuated with moments of laughter, tickling his neck, heating along his skin. Her cheek landed between his shoulder blades. The desire to spin around and find himself face-to-face with her...he barely resisted.

But he knew better. Evan would never get that door shut if he opened it with Addie. She'd slip in too easily. He'd fall too easily. It wasn't the falling part that concerned him. It was what came after that...the staying. The making a relationship work. His parents certainly hadn't given him a good example of that. How Jace had figured it out when he hadn't... Evan didn't have a clue. His track record was zero for two regarding the last women he'd dated. Zero for three if he counted the first time around with Addie.

He inched slowly toward the kitchen opening, Addie still tucked behind him, scrambling his senses with every step. It was a wonder he didn't smack into a wall.

When they were just about to freedom, one bird took off from its perch and beelined for the other.

"Go," he said, and Addie peeled away from him—regrettably—her squeal echoing down the hall. The bathroom door slammed just as Sawyer and Belay pounded down the stairs. "Oh no." And Evan had thought things couldn't get any crazier. "Belay, no!"

His command didn't even get an acknowledgment. Three stairs from the bottom, Belay jumped into the chaos. She went nuts, barking, leaping, chasing the birds around and around the living room. She wasn't close enough to catch them, just to send the animals into an absolute tizzy.

Sawyer shrieked, hands over his ears. Probably to protect himself from his own volume level. When Belay's chasing caused a bird to dive near Sawyer, his freak-out increased.

Evan swooped in and scooped Sawyer up under his left arm. After three loops around the living room, he managed to catch Belay by the collar with his right. All the while the birds screeched and zipped overhead.

Addie appeared in the entrance to the kitchen as Evan was dragging and carrying his two charges outside. Trying to move Belay was like trying to lug a dead vehicle through a patch of dirt. She was creating as much force as she could to stay in the bird zone, her body and limbs heavy, determined.

"Is this why you failed your guide-dog training? Was it the birds?" Belay knocked him off-kilter, and Evan took a second to steady himself. Usually she was what balanced him.

He left Sawyer on the porch with Addie and continued down the steps to his car, opened the back and forced Belay inside, shutting the door. She spun in circles, barking.

"You're okay, girl. Calm down. You can come back inside in a minute." After he set the birds free.

Evan returned to the porch. Addie was bent over, hands on her knees, as if catching her breath—from laughter and not the sprint outside, he assumed. She looked up, confirming his guess, her pretty brown cheeks creased.

"Are we going to have to call someone to get those things out of there?"

"No. We'll figure it out."

"I'm not so sure about that. You totally sacrificed me to the birds in order to protect yourself."

"I didn't *sacrifice* you. They just took me by surprise."

She laughed so hard she leaned against the porch railing to steady herself. Sawyer was peering in the front window of the house, jabbering about the birdies, thankfully not trying to go back inside.

"I'm glad you're so amused by my bird skills."

"More like you have no bird skills."

"Neither do you!"

"Yeah, but I admitted that right away. You tried to act all tough about it." Addie kept giggling, and the sound was messing with him. Making him think about kissing her. About all sorts of off-limits things. Addie could tie him up in knots without even trying. She took on the world—like remodeling and opening the B & B—without hesitation. She looked downright irresistible in work clothes. She laughed so hard she had to run for the bathroom. She had said *babies*, right? Evan hadn't just heard that wrong? But then she'd corrected herself right away. Likely she'd just been jumbled from the situation and making a blanket statement. *That's what happens when you have babies.* It sounded like something any mom would say. It was just…it had made him think about their pregnancy scare that summer.

What would it have been like if Addie had been pregnant? Would they have stayed together? Or would things have imploded between them? How would they have ever handled a pregnancy at their young ages? Especially after his accident when he hadn't been able to work.

It was good that things had happened the way they had. It was just… Evan couldn't help but think that she wouldn't have married her ex had the scare turned out to be legit.

But that would mean she also wouldn't have Sawyer.

And the little guy was worth the turmoil Addie had been through. No doubt about that.

"I'll look up what to do." Thankfully his phone was in his pocket. And thankfully he'd gotten his leg reattached before the bird fiasco. He scrolled through some posts. "Okay. Sounds like we should lower the blinds so they don't fly into a window and then we should make everything dark except for the exit."

"We." Addie cringed. "You mean, *you're* going to try that, right?"

His head swung even as his mouth bowed. "Right. That's exactly what I meant."

For all of Evan's fears and inadequacies over relationships, for all of the knowledge that he wasn't equipped to make one work for the long haul, if this morning was any representation of one, he'd be strangely content with that. Because every escapade with Addie was better than anything without her.

## Chapter Ten

It took them ten minutes to get the birds out of the house.

The floor, on the other hand, was going on eight hours with no end in sight. Evan had been right to doubt their expertise in taking on a project of this size. It might kill them both.

Addie slipped off the mask protecting her nose and mouth from the endless amounts of dust. "Sawyer needs to go down for the night." She paused her machine and leaned against it as if she might fall over without the support.

"That's fine. We should probably call it quits. Go at it again tomorrow."

Addie's nose wrinkled at his suggestion as she scanned the floor. It definitely wasn't done at a professional level, and there was a lot left to go.

They both moved into the kitchen, where

Sawyer and Belay were hanging out—Sawyer drawing at the table, Belay snoozing at his feet, cramped amidst all of the living room furniture they'd shoved into the space.

"Time for bed, buckaroo." Addie scooped him up from the bench.

"No-no-no." Sawyer's head shook with a vengeance. "I not tired!"

"Well, I am," Addie retorted.

"I put you to bed, Mommy." They laughed at Sawyer's offer.

"I would happily take you up on that, but Mommy has more work to do." Evan resisted a groan. Addie planned to continue? It was eight o'clock. They'd only stopped for sustenance twice today. His body was done. His everything was done.

And there was no way Addie didn't need a break.

"I want Eban. Eban put me to bed." Sawyer squirmed in Addie's arms, then lunged.

Evan caught the boy midleap, and Sawyer's little arms roped around his neck, clinging. How was he supposed to resist?

He silently asked Addie questions. *What do you want me to do? Hand him back? Get out of your hair? Help?*

"Do you mind putting him to bed with me? It might prevent a tantrum if we give in."

"No problem." Evan followed Addie to the back of the house. They swung by the bathroom, where she quickly brushed Sawyer's teeth.

Despite his protest in the kitchen, Sawyer crawled right into his bed, which was a small mattress on the floor against the wall. The space was obviously too tight for an additional bedframe. Addie sat on the mattress with him, and Evan perched on the side of the double bed.

"Remember, you only get to sleep in a big boy bed if you stay in it." Addie's admonition to Sawyer was frayed at the edges—as if it had been used on repeat for every nap and bedtime. She turned to Evan, her explanation quiet. "He started climbing out of his crib back in Michigan, so it hadn't been worth moving it."

"Shocking." His droll tone earned quirked lips from her.

"I knowed, Mommy," Sawyer piped up. "I be good."

"What should we thank God for today, Sawyer?"

"Belay." He pulled the blanket up under his chin. "And Eban and Mommy and me."

Being included in the grateful list wrenched a smile from Evan's tired body. Addie said a quick prayer, adding in a few requests for safety and provision.

Evan knew Addie didn't consider herself a veteran Christian—their conversation outside church had communicated as much—but it was good to see her softening in that arena. She'd talked about God freely with him while renovating today, asking questions, admitting doubts. She especially struggled with the concept of grace. Evan understood that. It didn't make any sense that God could love a person despite all of their sins. It didn't make any sense that God would exchange His perfect son for a fallen people. And yet, that's exactly what he'd done. Evan's conversation with Addie told him she accepted that truth logically. He just wasn't sure if she did emotionally yet.

But the truth was the truth whether feelings followed or not.

"Good night, bugaboo." Addie kissed Sawyer's forehead and hugged him. But instead of staying put, he scrambled out of bed.

He threw himself at Evan—as he had a tendency to do. Sawyer seemed to barrel into anything and everything.

Evan wrapped arms around the little guy. "Good night, Sawyer." His heart. He hadn't known it could expand like that.

They left Sawyer snuggled under his blankets with the door open an inch, hallway light on.

At the front of the house, Belay had gone back to snoozing under the breakfast-nook table.

"This has been a long day. We'll go at it again tomorrow." The number of sweeps they were having to do with different grits of sandpaper were more exhausting than climbing Mount McKinley.

"Sure." Addie took a swig from her water bottle. Didn't meet his eyes.

"You're like Belay when she's done something wrong and is evading punishment."

Her lips crept up. "I just…this is a way bigger project than I expected. I *have* to get it done."

She wasn't going to listen to him, and she was pushing herself too hard. There was no reasoning with her. Evan strode to the front door and exited onto the porch.

"Where are you going?" Addie called.

He didn't stop to answer. Maybe if she got curious enough, she'd follow.


Where had Evan disappeared to? Addie slowly walked in his wake and then peeked outside.

He was sitting on the hood of his car, leaning back against the windshield, arms tucked behind his head.

Strange. She stepped onto the porch. "What are you doing?"

"Breathing something besides dust."

"Can't you wreck your vehicle doing that? Dent it or something?"

"Nah. My car already has some hail damage and plenty of nicks and scrapes. I've never been a car guy. It's just a way to get around."

She moved closer, pausing at the side of the hood. Evan had donned a sweatshirt since it was cool out, especially with the rain they'd gotten earlier in the evening. A blanket lay heaped next to him.

"Is that for me?"

He studied the sky. "Maybe."

Addie wrapped herself in it, then climbed up and scooted backward, settling against the windshield like Evan. The cool metal and glass slithered through the blanket. Inside she'd been so warm from the physical labor. Sanding floors was no joke.

The night sky glittered and sparkled without the interruption of city lights, and Evan was right—suddenly her lungs could function again. "Wow."

"Exactly."

"So this is part of why you do all of the outdoorsy stuff, huh?"

Evan's answering chuckle warmed her more than the blanket.

For a couple of minutes, they simply sat.

Addie took deep breaths, concentrating on releasing her bunched muscles. Her shoulders were so tight they felt tied to her ears.

"Do you ever think about what-ifs?" Evan's out-of-the-blue question was like asking if she ever thought about Sawyer. Or money. Or how she was going to make the B & B successful.

"Yep. You're trying to distract me from working on the floors, aren't you, Evan Hawke?"

"Maybe." His grin was irresistible. "What do you think our lives would have turned out like if we'd been allowed to talk past that summer?"

Oy. "So different." Addie wouldn't have lived with guilt and shame as her constant companions. If Evan had known about Eli, then they'd have been able to make the decision to place him with a more equipped family together.

"Your parents were pretty strict about us."

*You don't even know the half of it.* Addie's soul ripped in two. She had to tell Evan about Eli, but when? How? Was this the moment? And if yes, what should she say?

Her next attempt to inhale stuttered, and her chest rose and fell like a toddler's attention span.

*Maybe I can do it in pieces.*

Some people ripped off Band-Aids when it was time for them to be removed, but Addie had always preferred a soak. Something to make it easier when she meticulously peeled away the edges, removing it as painlessly as possible.

Maybe she could do that with Evan. Maybe she could start revealing pieces of what happened instead of dumping all of it on him at once.

"I didn't want to stop talking to you. They made me. You know that, right?"

"I gathered that from the message you sent." The words were heavy, wounded even. "I even understood their demands at the time. I had a lot to work through myself. But it would have been nice to be able to communicate as friends once in a while. To know how you were."

"I felt exactly the same way." Addie would have given anything to know how Evan was faring, how his recovery was going, if he missed her like she'd missed him.

"I tried reaching out to you a couple of months after. Just as friends, because I didn't want to disregard your parents' wishes, but the number was no longer in service."

"That's because the phone had been disconnected."

His curiosity was palpable. "Why?"

"When I returned home that summer, my parents found out what we'd been up to." Even admitting that little bit filled her mouth with a metallic taste and sent a shudder through her.

Because it was one step closer to Evan knowing everything. To Evan loathing her. To Evan crumbling with remorse and anger over what he'd view as himself abandoning a child when it so obviously hadn't been a decision he'd made.

Evan groaned and rubbed hands over his face. "That's terrible. How?"

"They read our texts. Saw them once I got home. I should have deleted them off my phone, but I hadn't been thinking." That was how her mom had confirmed her suspicions regarding Addie's bouts of morning sickness.

"No wonder your parents had such an awful impression of me. They don't even know me, and I'm…" Air huffed from him. "I'm sorry that you had to go through that alone. I should have been there to shoulder that with you. I'm sure they were disappointed."

*If only.* If only Addie could have reached out to Evan at that time.

"They were upset with me—you know my parents were strict—but they also blamed you because you were older. I'm not sure why that meant it was all on you, but…" She squeezed the blanket closer, tighter. "They forbade me from talking to you anymore. They changed my number. Watched everything I did at the house."

"I looked up your home phone number and

called a few months after you'd left Colorado. Left a couple of messages. Did you know that?"

"No." Addie's eyes blurred, the lids crashing down. What if she'd been home? What if she would have answered? Would she have blurted out that she was pregnant? "They never told me. They literally cut me off from you."

An owl hooted in the distance.

"So that's why you didn't come stay with Alice and Benji the next summer. Because of me." His observation came out flat, dejected.

"Yep." *That and the fact that I'd just given birth to our son.* If only the words would fall off her tongue. But she was locked up tight. Revealing any of this to Evan was incredibly hard. She'd lived under the weight of fear and shame for so long, Addie couldn't shuck it off with one attempt.

*Baby steps. There's nothing wrong with baby steps. You still have time. Evan isn't going anywhere. Yet.*

"So, what happened to you after we were cut off that summer?" she asked.

"Well, it took me forever to get myself to functioning again."

It was a check in the column to support the crazy decision her parents had made, but Addie refused to accept the way they'd orchestrated and controlled the situation and her.

"Like how long?"

"'Bout a year and a half. I was angry for a long haul. And then, eventually, I just had to get out of there. Get away from the bitter kid I'd become." Remorse weighted down the admission.

"I went to bitter-town for a while." After giving birth to Eli, Addie had stopped attempting to follow any rules and leaped into the deep end. "I started drinking my senior year, hoping it would numb…everything." Her skin flushed, hidden in the shadows.

"Did it work?"

"No."

"And then I had a string of terrible boyfriends, which drove my parents up the wall. They got stricter. I got angrier. Eventually I got a job and moved out, found a stupid group of friends. I met Rex. I'm still not sure what we were thinking getting married. He was like the king of all my bad decisions. He was pretty much a jerk from the start." But Addie had made so many choices she'd regretted that she'd been determined, somehow, to make a marriage work.

"And then there's Sawyer," Evan offered.

All of her regrets melted. How could something so good come from so many mistakes? How could God give her such a gift when she didn't deserve it? Grace. That was the answer that kept boomeranging back to her. She didn't deserve Sawyer. Didn't *deserve* anything.

"Sometimes I feel like he's the only thing I've ever done right, and yet, I've messed up with him so many times. I always hoped I'd be a good mom. And then I became one, and every one of my glaring issues came to light. Sometimes I lose it over the smallest thing that doesn't even make sense, and other times I have the patience of Job. Sometimes I find Sawyer adorable and funny and sweet and other times I just want him to go to sleep at night so that I can have a moment to myself. I want to be perfect for him but I'm definitely not."

"No one is. But from what I see, you do a great job with him. He's happy and well-adjusted. You just made a big move and he's taking it all in stride."

Her laugh was scornful. "Right. Stride like running from me every time he gets the chance. I think the worst part about stuff like that is that I fear everyone around is going to think I'm a bad mom. That I don't have it all together. Or that maybe I'm ruining him because I've taken on a project this size. What if we fail, Evan? What if I do what the last owners did and run the place into the ground?"

"You've told me numerous times that you did the research and the math on the B & B."

"I have. I did. But what if it's not enough?" If something—anything—went wrong, she'd be in a mess of trouble.

"Then you just have to trust that it's going to be okay. You're halfway there. Look at how far you've already come. You're talking to Charlie, seeking advice. You're sticking to your budget. You're doing the right things. Beyond that is just a vast sea of things you can't control."

A jackhammer chiseled away at her temple. "Yes. But that part is so hard. I often think that I shouldn't have taken a risk like this. If I'd have saved the money I inherited instead of using it on the down payment, then Sawyer and I would have a nest egg right now. We'd have a safety net instead of—" she motioned to the house "—this."

"I can't tell you that you made the perfect decision." Evan's tone was contemplative. "But now that you're here, I'd have to say that you're where you're supposed to be. Whether you just learn from all of this or whether you turn the B & B into a raging success. Whatever happens, I believe that you and Sawyer will still be okay. You'll find a way, just like you have the years before this."

*Oh, Evan. Why are you being so nice to me? You're the last person who should be encouraging me, extending me grace.* And yet, this man believed in her, cheered her on. Just like Tito and Tita used to.

"You're too good to me, Evan Hawke."

The corner of his mouth lifted. "You're pretty hard on yourself, Addie Ricci."

He was right. She had been beating herself up for a long time. But telling Evan about Eli was only going to compound her guilt, not ease it. She would be causing him so much pain, and that thought haunted her.

"Anyone can see you're a good mom, Addie." Evan reached over and squeezed her knee. He let go quickly, but her cells still jumped to attention. "A very good mom. Don't let anyone else's opinions tell you different. And don't confuse taking a risk on the B & B with how much you love your kid, because I'm certain he's a majority of the reason you made this decision anyway."

True. "Thank you." Her gratitude came out whisper quiet. She'd needed to hear everything Evan just had to say—especially about the kind of mother she was. She just hadn't ever expected those words to be coming from Evan Hawke.

Evan followed Addie back inside the house to collect Belay. He hoped his impromptu break would be enough to convince her she was exhausted, and they could tackle the floors again tomorrow.

His hopes were dashed when she admitted she was going to work for "just a few more minutes."

Which would turn into hours.

Evan would like to command the woman to go to bed instead of continuing, but he did not see that going well. His only other option was to stay.

"Okay. Then let's get back to it." He strode into the living room, muscles whining, and snapped the mask back on.

"Evan!" Addie followed him into the space. "Go home. Please."

He switched the edger on. Motioned to his ear as if he couldn't hear. "What?"

She rolled her eyes. Crossed her arms. Generally looked more adorable than any woman had a right to. Evan ignored her and started to work. After about thirty seconds, she gave in and went back to her sander. The hum of the machines filled the house for a long while.

It was probably a good thing they were back at the floors. If Evan went home right now, he'd no doubt lie awake thinking about that conversation with Addie. About her parents. He cringed. They must have been so angry with him. They'd definitely been hard on Addie. Evan hated that she'd had to handle that alone. He should have been there for her. Should have made sure she was okay after the text that had separated them.

Addie flipped her machine off and threw her hands in the air. "Why won't it even out?" She flung her face mask across the room.

Evan turned off his edger and removed his mask. Silence reigned, though his ears continued with their own buzzing from the constant noise.

He inspected the space. "It's getting better." Wasn't it? They'd been through various grits of sandpaper at this point. And Addie was right, some spots were still crowned or uneven or dark. Evan had never sanded or refinished hardwood floors before, and after this, he'd never do it again. This floor needed a professional, but Addie didn't have the money for that, and he knew better than to sweep in and rescue her any more than he already was. Not that she'd even accept that.

"What was I thinking?" Pathetic tears zipped down her cheeks like a downpour. A couple plunged off her chin and plopped to the floor, leaving dots in the dust from their sanding.

*This is why I thought we should sleep and start again tomorrow.* By the grace of God, Evan didn't say that out loud. "It's going to be okay. We'll figure it out." Somehow.

"But it's a mess! And I don't have the money to hire someone! How can we refinish it if we can't get that stuff off? Or sand it flat?" She scrubbed fingers through her hair, loosening her ponytail.

"Look how much we got done today. It's just going to take time."

She let out a wail and covered her face with her hands. So much for his little pep talk.

What was he supposed to do? Seeing her standing in the middle of the mess sobbing was killing him.

Evan crossed over to her but left a ruler length between them. "Adelyn Ricci, it's going to be okay."

"No, it's not." The muffled declaration sounded like a little kid throwing a tantrum.

Evan's lips itched to curve. But that would most definitely get him into trouble. Instead, he moved into her space—into the place he wanted to be so badly but knew better than to be. He wrapped arms around her, drawing her against his chest. Without hesitation, she burrowed in, sniffling and mumbling about time and money and projects, moisture seeping into his T-shirt.

She felt so good tucked inside his arms. "Honey, I promise we'll figure it out. Tomorrow. After we both sleep. Okay?"

Those sweet brown eyes peered up at him as if he had the power to make everything better. And nothing made Evan want that more.

## Chapter Eleven

*What can I bring tonight?* Addie texted Charlie before pulling out of her driveway.

She and Sawyer were heading over to her place for a working dinner this evening. A crash course in social media, because Addie was rather inept in that area. Not that she'd had a lot of time to devote to it. But her minimal effort—coached by Charlie—had included a couple of hashtags and a discount she'd offered in order to fill up for Old Westbend Weekend. Two of the rooms were now booked for the whole week. Reservations had begun sliding in for after that also. Charlie had helped her offer a discount for the most immediate weeks she needed to fill and add a page to her website that included last-minute sales and deals. She'd said a newsletter would be next, but Addie was a slow learner when it came to technology. One cyber step at a time for her.

Her phone dinged when she was at a deserted stop sign, so Addie checked it before continuing. Nothing. I've got everything. Just come!

Are you sure? I could bring dessert. Not that she had time to cook, but she could pick something up.

The number of eye-rolling emojis that came back made her laugh.

Okay. You win. See you soon.

Charlie had been an absolute answer to prayers that Addie hadn't even thought to utter. And yet, answers were dropping into her lap.

God must really want her to see Him working in their lives. And she could. She did. "I see You," she said out loud as she drove, momentarily casting her vision toward the sky. "Thank You."

"I see you too, Mommy," Sawyer crowed from the backseat, where he was strapped into his car seat.

Addie laughed.

Now if God could just give her the strength and wisdom to figure out how to tell Evan about Eli. How to not wound him beyond measure by having unknowingly re-created his childhood. *Please, God.* The request was constantly on her mind.

She turned toward Evan's mom's house. They'd left plenty of time to swing by there on the way to Charlie's. He wanted her to check out the tile he'd used in the bathroom at his mom's. Evan said it was simple and affordable, and he'd help her if she wanted to do the bathroom upstairs that attached to the Monarch Room. And it could *really* use a redo.

The man was also turning out to be an answer to prayer. After her breakdown about the hardwood floors last week, he'd shown up the next day and worked tirelessly with her to get the floors done right. Eventually it had been good enough. The black spots hadn't completely disappeared, but, as Evan had pointed out, that's exactly where the end table would go. So they'd sanded and sanded, finally calling it all good. Then they'd cleaned up the mess, making sure to do an immaculate job before applying the finish, which had taken them into Wednesday.

The floors looked gorgeous, and there was no way Addie would have been able to do them without Evan. He'd saved her. Big-time.

After that, Evan had gone back to working on his mom's place. He hadn't contacted her for thirty-six hours. Not that she'd been counting or anything. It had been strange though.

He'd switched from being with her constantly to disappearing. Addie hadn't bugged him during that time, and he hadn't called or texted her. Then suddenly on Friday he'd landed back in her world, offering to help again.

In the last few days, they'd painted the remaining bedrooms and moved the furniture into the spaces. Addie had also cleaned and ordered products. The list of what they'd accomplished in the last week blew Addie's mind. Without Evan, she would have been like the last owners who'd defaulted and been crushed under the weight of the B & B. Evan had saved her until she was no longer treading on the water, but sitting on the shore, watching and listening to the beautiful waves crash. Addie had a list of things left to do, yes. And this week would be crazy, yes—she'd been calling it crunch week, and it would be. But for once, she could see the finish line. There was, most definitely, a light at the end of the B & B tunnel. Because of Evan Hawke.

Aspens lined the street Evan's mom's house was on, showing off their new spring greenery. The bushes outside the house were blooming, and the place had been painted a light buttercream—within the last few years, it looked like.

Addie got out of the car as Evan came down the front steps. "It looks so great!" she called, then released Sawyer from his car seat. He scrambled out, running straight into Evan, thankfully not knocking him over, hugging him, then calling out for Belay, who'd also come to greet them.

"Thanks." Evan's smile scrambled her insides as he met her by the car. Ever since their marathon floor-sanding session, something had changed between them. That attraction that had been buried under the surface had been rising up for big gulps of air, making itself known. She'd dressed in skinny jeans, flats and a striped shirt for dinner at Charlie's. It felt good to be out of working clothes. It felt even better to see Evan's eyebrows lift in appreciation. "You look nice."

"Thank you."

"It's good to see you taking a night off."

"It's a working dinner. Charlie's helping me with some social media and website stuff, but it's still good to get out of the house."

"I'm glad she's so much of a help."

"Me too. I seem to be surrounded by people like that lately." She flashed a pointed smile.

Evan shrugged. "It's nothing." It wasn't, and they both knew it. "Come on. I'll give you a tour."

Just like Evan to change the subject away from himself. Addie wasn't sure how he was going to survive the Old Westbend Weekend hometown-hero role. He'd probably melt into a puddle of embarrassment on the stage.

Inside, the place was immaculate. Addie popped her head back outside. "Sawyer, you stay right by the house with Belay, okay?" No way did he need to come inside and mess anything up.

"Okay, Mommy!"

"I'm still going to have to keep an eye on him," she told Evan.

"Agreed."

The front window in the living room gave her a great view of the two playing, so Addie relaxed a bit. She listened as Evan told her what he'd done to get it ready to sell, pride evident.

"When is it going on the market?"

"Tomorrow."

"That's great. It's going to sell so fast."

They checked on Sawyer again, moving him and Belay into the fenced backyard before heading for the bathroom. Evan was right—the tile was very plain, but that could be a good thing. It would be more timeless that way, and Addie could always bring in color with towels or flowers and decorations.

"It helps to see it done. You're pretty impressive, Evan, that you can do all of this."

His lips bowed. "Now you sound like Jace.

He's lost when it comes to fixing pretty much anything on a house. But then, I don't have the knack with animals or people that he does."

"Oh, I'm not sure I agree with that." Addie had seen Evan at church yesterday but hadn't spoken to him because so many people had demanded his attention. He might be on the quieter, get-me-out-of-here side when it came to social settings, but he could hold his own. And his huge, generous heart was recognizable from miles away.

They traveled back into the living room and Addie stepped outside to check on Sawyer. He'd found a stick and was running around the yard with it, Belay on his heels. She wanted to tell him not to run with the stick—the number of bad scenarios she could imagine happening stacked up like piles of laundry in her mind— but she clamped her jaw shut. No matter how much she'd like to protect him from injury or harm, she had to let him be a boy. Had to let him run wild and free from time to time. Especially with how much he'd been cooped up during the B & B facelift.

Addie sank to a seat on the back steps, and Evan joined her. "I like the tile. Now I just have to figure out if I can do it. Any idea how much I'd need for that bathroom?"

"I measured yesterday." Evan plugged some

numbers into the calculator on his phone. "I think you could get the tile for around this." He showed her a number that was way lower than she'd expected. "I've got some extra pieces here for filling in, and some leftover grout too." He set his phone next to him on the step. "With free labor, that's really not bad."

"Why is that?"

"That the price isn't bad?"

"No. That the labor is free." Addie let herself look long and hard at this man who was rescuing her one day at a time when she hadn't even known she'd needed to be rescued. She understood why he'd started helping her in the beginning. But now? "You've paid your single-mom dues, Evan. Why are you sticking around? This is over and above." She was confused…and she was falling for him all over again.

Not smart given their situation.

Sawyer yelped as he tumbled, thankfully tossing the stick to the side as he rolled. He popped back up, brushing off his jeans. "I okay!" He retrieved the stick again and then broke into a sprint.

"I should tell him not to run with that, right?"

Evan's mouth curved while watching Sawyer, and she fell a little more. "He'll be all right. He just handled that, didn't he?"

True.

Evan's heated gaze landed on her, filled with the electrical current of an impending thunderstorm. "It's not about honoring my mom anymore. I just can't seem to *not* help you out. You're like a bug zapper and I'm a fly. There's no turning away from the light."

Addie laughed. "I'm not sure whether to be flattered or offended."

Evan found her hand, tugged it to his lap, squeezed and held on. Warning sirens flashed, but she didn't pull back. "I know we were young in high school, but it actually meant something to me. *You* meant something to me."

One half of her was delighted and warmed and flattered that Evan was admitting he cared for her and about her. But the other half knew it was the last complication she needed—or deserved—right now.

"You meant something to me too." Addie told herself that saying it in past tense made it acceptable. But it wasn't just past tense. She cared about him now. Too much. She couldn't allow herself to fall for him when he didn't know about Eli. And certainly, once he found that out, he'd want nothing to do with her.

She slipped her hand free, and it landed back on her own lonely lap with all of the excitement of a teenager on finals day. Evan didn't say anything more. Didn't push. They sat in silence as Sawyer zoomed by them.

The temperature was in the high fifties today. With the sun hiding behind clouds, Addie shivered. Evan got up, went inside and returned with a zip-up hoodie. He put it around her shoulders, and she barely resisted burrowing into the thing and never coming out. It smelled woodsy and clean and comforting—like Evan.

"Well, I do know one thing." He dropped back down to the step next to her.

"What's that?"

"We've been working way too hard, and we're due for some ice cream."

She hadn't been expecting that.

Sawyer flew their way. "Ice cream, ice cream!" he chanted, landing in front of the two of them, his grubby hands on one of each of their knees. Of course he'd heard the quietly said comment from a mile away.

"We have to be at Charlie's at six o'clock."

Evan checked the time on his phone, showing her. "What do you say?"

They could fit it in. And now that Sawyer had heard the option existed, there'd be no changing his mind.

"Ice cream before dinner, huh? I see why the kids like you, Evan Hawke."

He stood and hauled her up with him. "Sawyer's about the only kid I know, and for some reason, he's decided I'm okay."

More than okay. Sawyer was very much hooked on Evan. He would miss the man like crazy when he went back to work, back to his home.

And Sawyer wasn't the only one.

*Do not get your hopes up, Addie Ricci. Evan's going to be wounded beyond belief when you tell him about Eli. He's not just going to forgive you and declare he's in love with you and that he wants to stay in town and give up his career for a divorcée with a toddler. One who kept a secret from him for the last ten years.*

No matter how much she might hope for that list of things, it wasn't going to come true. The opposite would. And then Addie would spend another decade attempting to get over the man when she'd never gotten over the boy.

"What is going on with you? You're a million miles away." Jace threw an unopened soda at Evan, and he caught it before it crashed to the floor. He was watching *Professional Bull Riding* with his brother, but his mind was anywhere but on the screen. He wasn't even sure what had just happened on the last ride.

"You're thinking about Addie, aren't you?" Jace dropped into the chair that flanked the couch in the living room of his and Mackenzie's cabin. Mackenzie was out with her niece Ruby, and Jace had taken a rare break from his EMT prep. "You looove her."

"You're five years old."

Jace flashed an unrepentant grin. "So what's the deal with her? You two were constantly together that summer and you've been spending an awful lot of time at the B & B lately."

Back in high school it had started out so simple. See girl. Get to know her. Fall for her. They were just missing the happily-ever-after part.

"You ever have one person you just can't figure out? Like they're your mystery person? The one who got away. Who you wondered about too much over the years?"

"Yep. I married her. Still don't have her figured out all the time though." He took a swig of soda. "Do you ever think that maybe you and I were just built for the first women we loved? That maybe seeing all that Mom and Dad went through…we refused to partake in that kind of drama and knew what we wanted when we saw it?"

Huh. "Can't say that I've ever thought of it that way." It was an interesting theory though. "Addie and I have a lot that's happened between us. It wasn't just some simple relationship we can pick back up like you and Mackenzie."

Jace snorted. "Simple. Right. That's not the word I would use."

"Well, you sure figured things out fast."

"Again, not a word I would use. When I first showed up at Wilder Ranch, Kenzie wanted to shoot me in the foot. Nothing about her hating me felt fast."

"Since you two are about the schmoopiest of the schmoopy, I'd say she got over her anger."

Jace laughed. "Most days." He leaned forward. "So if things are so complicated, what exactly happened?"

"After my surgery, when she went back to Michigan, her parents didn't let us talk anymore. They'd found out we'd been…" This was harder than he'd thought it would be to admit to his little brother. Especially since he'd always wanted Jace to be able to look up to him. But Evan certainly hadn't been perfect. He wished he and Addie would have waited. They'd been so young to make a choice like that. He hated looking back and knowing he'd been part of that impatience. "Fishing in the dark."

"Ah."

"On the morning of my accident, Addie told me she thought she might be pregnant." The last word detonated like a bomb.

Jace's jaw unhinged. "Woah."

"Exactly. She tried to blame herself for my

accident just like you did, but it was nobody's fault but mine. A couple of days after the amputation, I asked her about the scare when I was still in the hospital." He'd been highly medicated but coherent enough to know they still had an issue if she was pregnant. "She told me it had been a false alarm."

"I didn't know any of that. And on top of all you were going through. That's a lot, E."

"Yeah. So I guess you could say that we don't have the simplest past."

"Who does? What about now?"

Now? Since the night they'd begun refinishing her floors, something had changed between himself and Addie, making Evan question everything. After they completed that project, Evan had backed away from her to create some space and talk sense into himself. But he'd only lasted from Wednesday night until Friday morning before contacting Addie again. She was his kryptonite. Currently he was locked in a battle over what to do—get out before he fell any further for her and potentially hurt both of them, or give in to his wants—kiss her, lean toward her, figure out if there was a chance he could be different this time around. If maybe he was less of a mess with Addie than he'd been with anyone else. But if he failed? They'd all suffer. Sawyer too.

The announcer's voice rose with excitement and the crowd cheered.

"You like her," Jace continued, this time in a more serious tone. "What's wrong with that? It wouldn't be the end of the world to fall for her and her kid and settle down near your brother, would it?"

Jace made it all sound so simple. But he wasn't broken like Evan. He'd probably been too young to remember all of the times Dad had sobered up for a week or two. A month. Even a couple months one time. Each episode had given Evan hope. And then the relapses had pounded into his psyche that his dad loved alcohol more than he loved them. That they weren't worth getting better for. That leaving first was the smart thing to do in a relationship, because then someone else couldn't destroy you. Not when you'd already taken care of that on your own.

"Of course I care about her. I always have. And I'm not denying my attraction to her. It's just…" So many things. "I don't even live here. And she does. So how would that ever work?" *Plus, I don't know how to do a relationship well. Somehow you got that gene when I didn't.* Just ask Evan's ex-girlfriend. She'd agree about his inadequacies when it came to relationships. And there'd been another situation too. Maybe not as serious, but likely just as hurtful.

"You could live here if you wanted to. Colorado has plenty of places for you to lead groups. Or this could be your home base while you travel instead of Chattanooga. I'd be just fine with having you around, even if you are annoying."

Evan laughed. Living near his brother wouldn't be the worst thing in the world. They were all each other had left of immediate family. Although, now Jace had Mackenzie. Evan was glad for that. She obviously loved Jace. Was a perfect match for his little brother.

And Jace was right—technically Evan could live in Colorado. No doubt Christopher could be convinced of the same since his wife's parents lived in Denver. It wasn't Evan's career that held him back from Addie. It was the same thing that had kept him from coming home too much or being in a relationship for too long.

He detached from people when things got serious. It didn't cut as deeply when you disconnected before the other person did. Or at least that's what Evan told himself. He wasn't even sure that was true…he'd just clung to it for a long time, unwilling to give up the idea. Something about it made him feel safe. In control. But of course he knew control was an illusion. Evan hadn't been able to stop his dad from choosing alcohol over them, he hadn't been able to stop his accident or amputation and he hadn't been able to stop Addie's parents from separating them. He couldn't direct the future either, but that didn't keep him from shutting down when his heart tried to get involved.

Evan was getting too close to Addie and Sawyer. If his past repeated itself, continuing things would only end in heartbreak. And yet, he couldn't seem to retreat or resist her. There was this new feeling inside him. One that wanted to keep pursuing. That wanted to see if he could change his crippled patterns.

For eons, Evan had been convinced he only had half a heart. And he still believed that to be true. But what if Addie was the other half of it?

## Chapter Twelve

Evan managed to hang out another hour with Jace before claiming exhaustion.

His fists strangled the steering wheel repeatedly on the drive home, his mind spinning. *Now isn't the time to be digging up questions that have messy answers. Or no answers at all. You need to go home and sleep on this.*

But just like his first visit to the B & B almost two weeks ago, Evan's vehicle had a mind of its own. Once again he felt like a stalker as he parked outside Addie's. Once again his logic was sorely lacking.

Was she awake? Plenty of ground-level lights were still on, so she must be. He'd left Belay at his mom's house tonight, but she'd be fine without him for a while longer. She was probably welcoming the night to herself. Or she was sitting by the front door, tail occasionally scraping across the floor, willing to forgive him the moment the key slipped inside the lock.

Option two was far more likely.

He took the steps slowly, still warring with himself, then knocked on the door quietly, not wanting to disrupt if Addie was sleeping. He heard noises inside, like a television was on, so he knocked again a little louder.

"Addie? It's Evan."

The front porch light flicked on. A second later the door opened two inches, the high chain she'd installed to circumvent any more of Sawyer's escapes still latched. She peeked out. "Evan? What's going on? Everything okay?" The door closed, unlatched, then reopened.

Not really, but how was he supposed to respond? He should have practiced on the way over, but it wouldn't have mattered, because he honestly wasn't sure what he wanted to say. *I think I like you but I'm scared out of my mind about it. How do you feel about me?* He resisted a snort. While he was at it, maybe he could leave a note with some boxes for her to check. *Yes. No. Maybe. No way. Smells funny. Not a fan of the facial hair.*

"I thought I'd…measure the bathroom again so that I can pick up that tile for you in the morning on my way over."

"I thought you already measured." Confusion filled her pretty face, which was devoid of makeup. She was in pajamas—flowered pants and a gray T-shirt—and her hair was wet, so she must have just gotten out of the shower.

"I did." Sure did. "I just wanted to double-check before buying the tile." Not that Herbert's wouldn't let him return a box if they bought one too many. Evan kept that tidbit to himself. "And then I thought I could tear some of it out tonight. Get prepped for tomorrow." He resisted wincing at the hefty stretch of why he was currently on her porch. This drop by was the equivalent of calling someone in the middle of the night and then hanging up. With caller ID.

"Okay, come in."

Evan stepped inside. He could add this visit to his list of stupid ideas. He should have listened to his more logical side and gone home. What was he going to do now? Ask her how she felt about him? And what if she said she had feelings for him too? What then? What if he still chickened out and ran? How could he do that to her and Sawyer?

He'd abandoned great relationships in the past. Why did he think he could be different now?

*You might be. You could be. Maybe. Maybe there's a statute of limitations on how long a dad can mess you up for.*

Addie studied him expectantly. "So…let's measure."

"I, ah, forgot my measuring tape." Could he sound more foolish right now?

Her forehead wrinkled. "Aren't your tools still sitting in the living room?"

"Oh. Yeah. Totally." He tried to laugh, but it came out as a wheeze. "I'll grab them." He escaped into the darkened room and ducked over the tool bag.

*Shouldn't have come*, his brain screeched. *Shut up, brain.* He gave it a mental kick into the corner. This whole scenario was so abnormal for Evan, so out of his comfort zone, that he feared his body might decide to shut down like a junky old phone.

He met Addie at the base of the stairs, tool bag in his grip. "Did I interrupt you? Thought I heard a TV on when I got here. Sorry to barge in on you like this."

"You're fine. I was just watching a tutorial about how to re-cover the breakfast-nook bench. I'm hoping to conquer that tomorrow."

Upstairs, the bathroom was small, and the tile surrounding the tub was brown and ugly, not to mention chipped. Stains permeated the grout in numerous spots. The tile from Herbert's wasn't going to be featured on HGTV anytime soon, but it would still brighten up the space.

Addie stood in the doorway while he measured. Again. And made notes on his phone. Again.

"Thank you. I'm not sure I can tell you that enough. You're saving my bacon on this place."

*And you're cooking mine. You've got me tied in knots, Addie Ricci. It's an uncomfortable place to be.* "You're welcome."

"How loud will the demo be? Because I'd like to not wake Sawyer."

"Shouldn't wake him. Not if he could sleep through us sanding the floors."

"True. Sleeping through anything is one of his better qualities. That and his hugs. They're so—"

"Committed." *Bad word choice, Hawke.*

"Exactly! To be honest, I've been afraid he was going to knock you off-balance a time or two. You're probably going to make fun of me for that silly thought, aren't you?"

"Actually…" he stretched the word out. "It's a legitimate concern. I've thought the same before."

She beamed as if she'd won a prize. "For once my apprehension regarding you is well warranted."

The measuring tape snapped shut, and Evan yelped. Blood oozed from the tender spot between his thumb and pointer finger.

Addie stepped in and captured his hand, inspecting. "Looks like you need a Band-Aid." Her touch was…he swallowed and yanked his hand back.

"I'm fine." And he'd been right—coming here had been a stupid idea.

Why had he ever thought he could be a different person than he had been in the past? History was doomed to repeat itself. No matter how much Evan wanted to prove it wrong.

One would think that a swarm of wasps had attacked Evan the way he'd jumped when she'd touched his hand. He was acting so strange tonight. Showing up at the B & B without warning while wearing clothes that were nicer than the paint-splattered ones he typically donned for manual labor. Saying he wanted to measure and demo but then forgetting his tools were here. Jumping when she moved the least bit into his space. And his *I'm fine* had been half growl, half desperation, scraping along her skin with equal parts attraction and curiosity.

*What's going on with you, Evan Hawke?*

"I've got some downstairs." Addie didn't wait for his protest, just headed for the bathroom on the main floor. She rummaged through the plastic bin that currently housed their supplies. She'd buried the Band-Aids because Sawyer considered them stickers and used them at every opportunity. Addie had begun telling him he couldn't use one without blood showing. And then had become afraid he'd do something to make that happen just to earn one. After setting a stack of items on the floor so she had better access, she found a box at the bottom of the bin. Covered in cartoon characters.

She chuckled. It would do.

*Clink clink clink* greeted her as she neared the upstairs bathroom. Evan was carefully chipping tile from the wall. Pieces were falling into the tub, shattering, making a huge mess. Addie would have liked to line the tub with a tarp first so that cleanup would be simpler, and it wasn't like Evan not to think of the same.

"You okay tonight? You seem off. Anything on your mind?"

"Nope. I'm fine." More tile disengaged from the wall.

She stepped fully into the small space, and it instantly shrank with the two of them filling it. "Here. I've got a Band-Aid."

"I really don't need one." He didn't turn to face her.

His shoulders were heavy with some burden. For once she'd like to be the one offering relief.

"Be a big boy and get your Band-Aid like a man, Evan Hawke."

She grabbed his elbow and turned him in her direction. He cast his vision toward the ceiling. Strange. Addie ignored his case of the crabbies and caught his hand again. The slice had clotted, and blood stained his skin. She rinsed the cut in the sink and poured some of the hydrogen peroxide over it that she'd also brought up. It bubbled and fizzed. That part always distracted Sawyer when he got injured. After drying it, she applied the Band-Aid.

"There. Good as new." With Sawyer, she would smooch the owie. Addie would not be doing that with Evan.

She glanced up. Evan wasn't looking at his hand or the bathroom demolition. His toasted-marshmallow eyes were lasered in on her.

Was he memorizing her lips? Or was that an illusion? He smelled good. Fresh. Like soap with a hint of sandalwood.

Despite their close proximity, he didn't inch back, didn't retreat. Her breath jammed in her throat. He was looking at her like he'd fight the whole world and deliver it on a platter if she asked. Like he…*oh my*. Like he cared about her. She recognized that expression from high school. Evan had never told her he'd loved her, but Addie had known. Just like she now knew why he'd arrived at the B & B tonight acting so peculiar.

*Oh, Evan.* Her heart tripped over itself in her chest. *You have no idea how much I care about you.* He was right in front of her, within reach and yet so, so far away. Tears pooled. It was time to tell him about Eli—Addie didn't have any other choice when she and Evan were both developing feelings for each other. She couldn't let that continue without honesty. But she would lose the best man she'd ever known when she did.

"Addie?" Evan's hands cradled her face, his thumbs catching moisture. Addie had never been so emotional—even through divorce or pregnancy. But remodeling and being in close contact with Evan were the two things, it seemed, that shoved her over the edge of that bluff. Along with the realization of what had to happen now. Couldn't she just go one more day without messing this up? Without ruining everything?

"Because this is probably never going to happen again, let me just—" She went up on her tiptoes and pressed her lips to his, and he answered—first with surprise, then surrender. Her whole body rushed with sensation, registering every nuance—the roughness of his stubbled cheeks, the way he moved into her, his hands switching to cover her lower back, tugging her close. She would give anything to live in this moment. When it all went away, this was what she would remember—that he'd cared about her, that he'd maybe even loved her again. Fleeting? Yes. But worth it. Every moment with Evan was.

His kiss was somehow urgent and careful at the same time. Sweet and tender and so Evan. His lips traveled to her cheeks, her forehead. "Why is this never going to happen again?"

*Because I'm about to break your heart, and I'm so so sorry.*

Evan cleared more tears from her cheeks with his weathered hands, nothing soft about them and yet everything soft about him. "Addie, what's going on? What is it, honey?"

The endearment about did her in.

*God, I didn't mean for it to happen, but I love this man. Maybe I always have. What I'm about to tell him is going to break him. Comfort him with that peace of Yours that Pastor Higgin talked about. The one that passes understanding. We're going to need it. He's going to need it.*

She and God might be new to each other, but He was getting the whole mess of Addie Ricci tonight. Supposedly He could handle all of her issues. She was certainly going to put that theory to the test.

"Let's go sit and I'll tell you."

Addie led him to the sofa in the living room, her hand shaking the whole time. Dread wrapped talons around Evan's windpipe, suffocating him. Something had to be seriously wrong. Any question he'd lobbed at her on the short trip to the living room had gone unanswered, causing alarms to fire along his nerves with each step.

She'd rearranged furniture once the floors were finished. Now the sofa flanked the middle of the north wall, two chairs facing it, the coffee table in the middle. Near the front window, Addie had created another nook with a small round table and two mismatched chairs. In case someone wanted to take their coffee or tea by themselves, she'd said.

Everything in the B & B exuded Addie's touch. She had a way of designing that made it feel like home. Evan could picture an older couple having tea in the afternoon or a family gathered around the dining table. Someone curled up in one of the chairs reading. Addie had made the B & B come back to life, and yet, her current facial expression was that of someone facing a devastating death.

He sat on one end of the sofa, but instead of sitting next to him, Addie retreated to the other end. Like that smoking kiss upstairs hadn't happened. Like she didn't want to be next to him. How could she kiss him like that and then retreat so quickly? Wasn't he supposed to be the runner?

She turned her body in his direction, tucking a knee underneath her, the middle cushion of the vintage—aka old but in good condition—sofa stretching between them like a 5K. "Can I ask you for one favor?"

Everything in him wanted to scream no. Everything in him said this conversation wasn't going to be one of the good ones. "Okay."

"I mean one more favor, I guess." He'd certainly granted her plenty in the time he'd helped her on the B & B, but he didn't regret any of them. Yet. "Would you hear me out? Will you listen to everything I have to say all the way through?"

"Sure." Why was she making this all sound so dire? Whatever she had to say or ask, she should just do it.

"That week you were in the hospital, after your accident." She studied her wringing hands. "It was one of the worst things I've ever experienced."

"Me too." So this was about them in the past, not the present?

"It was excruciating watching you suffer."

Evan's mouth reached for a curve despite the topic. "It was excruciating suffering."

Addie's attempt at a responding smile crashed

and burned. "Right. Well, I freaked out a bit after your accident, seeing you struggle so much. That's why, when you asked me about the pregnancy scare, I said it had been simply that. A scare." Her words rushed like a mountain stream over slippery rocks. Evan had to lean in to catch everything. "But the truth is, I didn't know that for sure. I just hoped that's what was going on. That stress was messing with my cycle. And I didn't see how letting you continue to worry was helping your recovery. So I said it was a false alarm when it actually… wasn't. And after I told you that, you started improving."

With each admission, each revelation, Evan's blood cooled and slowed. It was like watching a program in another language and trying to piece together the gist of it. "It was a huge relief at the time. I didn't know how I'd take care of you or a kid. Especially not after the accident. But…what are you saying? That you were pregnant? Or just didn't know that you weren't at that time?"

Had that sentence made any sense? Evan wasn't sure what he was saying. Or what she was saying.

Addie pushed out a long exhale. "When I went home to Michigan, I started throwing up in the mornings. My mom found our texts, and

she put it together that I was, indeed, pregnant.
She forced me to go to the doctor, and they confirmed it."

A wounded sound slipped from Evan's throat.
"What?" The word snapped into the quiet. "Are
you saying you were pregnant with our baby
when you left Colorado and you didn't tell me?"

Addie swiped at tears that were free-flowing
down her cheeks. The space his lips had occupied only minutes ago. Back when he'd had
hope. Back when Addie had been a possibility. Back when he'd thought he knew her, could
trust her.

"That's exactly what I'm saying."

## Chapter Thirteen

Addie had been pregnant at sixteen years old...
because of him. She'd been so young. Evan
wanted to go back and throttle the teenage version of himself. *God, what did we do?* They'd
been playing with fire, and they'd sent a forest
up in flames. Emotion built behind Evan's eyes,
and he blinked repeatedly to fight it.

Where was this child of theirs? Had something happened? "But you don't have a kid
who's nine. Only Sawyer. So... I don't understand." Evan had entered a twilight zone. Either
that, or he was about to wake up and realize this
was all a dream. Or a nightmare. In all of his
imaginings over what Addie might tell him, her
admitting that she'd actually been pregnant that
summer when she left Colorado wasn't even a
contender on the list.

It was impossible. It didn't make any sense.

Addie wouldn't have kept something like that from him. Evan couldn't deal with the current news until he had all of it laid out in front of him. Every tendon in his body begged him to get up and sprint or pace or run. He forced them all into submission, a quiet hum of agitation coursing through him.

"My parents were incredibly upset." She swallowed. "Incredibly." Addie stood and began pacing the length of the couch, behind the two chairs facing it. The redone floors creaked under her steps, showing their age. Evan was strangely jealous of her movement. If he pushed off the couch right now, he was afraid he'd walk out the front door without hearing her out. She had asked him for that, but currently, he was staying purely for himself and the information only she could fork over. "My dad especially. He was irate. He blamed you because you were older. I told him it wasn't your fault, that we'd both made decisions, but he didn't listen."

Evan agreed with her dad. His stomach rolled and pitched.

"I told my parents that we needed to tell you about the pregnancy. That once you were removed from the accident by a few weeks or even months, that you would be able to handle the news."

She was being generous. Even months after

the accident, Evan would have lost his mind if Addie had told him she was, in fact, pregnant. He would like to think he'd have pulled himself together and supported her, figured things out. But his track record at that time had been dismal. It had taken him over a year to calm the anger and injustice over his accident and longer to begin figuring out how to live again.

Addie wasn't waiting for him to comment or urge her on. She was lost in her own torment right now. Her fists were tight, her eyes—which could usually hold his attention for days—were hollow and lost. Her gaze flitted by him as if afraid to land.

A cry sounded, distraught, sleepy. Addie paused, listening. When another came, she held up a finger. "I'll be right back."

When she scooted from the room, Evan dropped his head into his hands. He couldn't even form a prayer. His mind was too jumbled. Too confused. It took her a hundred years to return.

"I'm sorry." She paused behind the chairs again, as if using them as a buffer between them. "Sawyer had a bad dream. When he gets overly tired, he tends to have more of them." She let out a rushed exhale. "Not that you need to know all of that. Okay, so, as I was saying, I wanted to tell you, but my parents disagreed.

They were so angry." That sentence dropped to a forlorn whisper. "They'd let me visit Tito and Tita, and I'd gotten myself pregnant. I'd ruined my junior year of high school, but they were determined it wouldn't stretch beyond that. They told me that if I reached out to you in any way, they'd cut me off. That if I tried to tell you I was pregnant, I'd be on my own. And then they orchestrated an adoption for our son."

"What?" Her parents had threatened her like that? And they'd forbidden her from even telling him about their baby? Was that even legal? How could all of this have happened and Evan didn't have a clue? He'd been walking around for years without knowing a child bearing his resemblance existed. It was too mind-boggling to handle. He couldn't sit still any longer. Evan shoved off from the couch, needing to move, needing to expel some of the injustice roaring through his veins.

He'd abandoned a kid and hadn't even known it. He'd done the same thing his father had done to him without being given the chance to undo history. He'd been a deadbeat dad. An absentee father. And Addie—and her parents—had made that happen.

Addie shrank into herself when he stopped in front of her. "I was sixteen and pregnant. I didn't know how to stand up to them. I couldn't get tossed out of their house or handle a pregnancy on my own. So I followed their orders." Pain carved into her features. "I only held our son once." Sobs racked her body, her anguish palpable. Evan backed up against the chair, his body sagging from the shock. He was not going to comfort her right now. Not going to reach for sympathy when Addie had basically stolen his child from him. "He lives in Michigan with his adoptive parents."

"I have a son." The words were foreign and heavy on Evan's tongue. Surreal. More painful than anything he'd ever experienced. "That's… I can't…but you." Evan attempted to swallow, but his body had abandoned that ability. "If you weren't allowed to tell me you were pregnant at sixteen, why didn't you contact me after? Or tell me right away when we ran into each other in town? How could you work beside me and not let that information out?" How could she have slaved on the B & B right next to him day after day? Laughed with him. Talked with him. About so many things. But not their son. Not their son.

Acknowledgment slammed into him, sending his chest and shoulders back as if someone had physically shoved him. Addie *had* let that information out. Accidentally. *Babies*. She'd meant that word. Addie had birthed not one, but two babies.

Two pregnancies. One being his kid. So she had told him—she just hadn't meant to.

Whatever Addie had to say from this point on didn't matter. Whatever came out of her mouth couldn't be trusted.

The only thing Evan was certain of was that life as he knew it had just ended.


"Evan, I promise I tried to find a way." *Please believe me. God, let him believe me.*

*But why should he?* her conscience asked.

Addie didn't have an answer for that. She only had this shaking, shoddy, weak body that wanted to curl into a ball. Her heart raced so fast she placed a hand over it to calm the stampede.

"I contemplated every scenario over and over again for months while I was pregnant and then the years after. I didn't know how to get to you when I lived with my parents. And once I moved out… I thought it was too late to tell you. That it would only cause you pain." *And I was right.* "I wanted to, but I was so ashamed of what had happened, I didn't know how. Every year on our son's birthday I wrote you a letter. And every year I didn't send it because I was mortified of what I'd let happen and frightened of what it would do to you." It all sounded so lame now that the truth was out. Evan was right. Addie should have told him long ago. But he didn't know what it was like to live under the weight of a lie she'd never agreed to.

"When we started working on the B & B, I was determined to tell you. But then you brought up Luc Wilder and how upset you'd be in that situation. And when you talked about fearing repeating your childhood, I just… I didn't know how to bring up our son without scarring you. I didn't want to be the one to make your nightmares come true."

Evan rubbed the heels of his hands against his eyes. "This isn't happening. This can't be happening." He bolted for the front door. She listened for his vehicle to start, but instead… It sounded like he'd lost whatever was in his stomach. In the bathroom, Addie located a washcloth and wetted it with cool water. She peeked in at Sawyer, who was now sleeping soundly again, his cheeks flushed and feathered with his long lashes. She might have done everything else wrong, but she'd raised a good son. Hadn't she? She stepped onto the porch with legs as shaky as baby tree branches.

Evan's fists were curled around the porch railing, and he was leaning against it as if he'd crumble without the support. Would he even accept the cloth from her?

Addie set it on his knuckles. He flinched. She moved out of his space, backing against the house, hands tucked behind her, throat grappling for saliva.

Lights from the town twinkled through the evergreens as if happily unaware of the turmoil currently resonating between Evan and her. A distant engine revved and then faded.

The front of the B & B taunted Addie with more work. The siding and porch would need to be redone at some point, but the projects would require money. She'd have to save for them. She'd been feeling so good about the B & B. So ready. But now it all felt huge again. Like a house built out of toothpicks that could crumble in a slight breeze.

After a minute, Evan scrubbed the washcloth across his face with so much agitation that she was surprised he didn't rip off skin. She resisted taking it from him and switching to gentle motions. She resisted every instinct she had right now, which was to go to him, to comfort him, to beg him for forgiveness. If she did any of that, she was afraid that his jumpiness upstairs over the cut on his hand would majorly pale in comparison.

Addie didn't want him to leave. If they could just talk things out—just land on some sort of understanding. The idea was lofty and far-fetched, but she was holding on to it like a toddler with her favorite toy.

Evan finally turned. His look—it was as if she was the lowest of the low. Like he didn't recognize her. And the wounding beneath squeezed the oxygen from her lungs. *Oh, Evan, I'm so sorry. I'm so sorry.*

Addie had always known this moment would be awful, but she'd never been able to picture exactly how it would go. With anger? Yelling? A fist through the wall? Evan was a mix of the first with a dash of seething thrown in.

She'd never before witnessed a better definition of the word.

With a distressed groan, he stalked down the porch and disappeared into the shadows as if he couldn't be near her, and yet, strangely, he didn't just leave. Maybe that meant he wanted to know more about what had happened or about their son. Maybe that meant they could continue the conversation.

She followed Evan into the darkness, not bothering with the porch light. Found him leaning back against the railing, head hanging low. What she wouldn't give to walk up and slip her arms around his waist. To comfort each other like they should have been able to do ten years ago.

"Evan, you have no idea how sorry I am. How

often I've relived that time, wondering what I should have done differently. How I could have reached out to you. What we would have done… I'm sorry I was so weak. That I didn't stand up to my parents. I'm sorry I didn't find a way to tell you after the fact. I'm sorry that your son was taken from you and you didn't have a choice. That you didn't know he existed. I'm sorry, I'm sorry, I'm sorry." Her whole body ached with the words. She meant them with every fiber of her being. If she could go back, if she could fix it. *If, if, if.*

Evan was frozen, unmoving.

"Say something. Please." Anything. She couldn't handle the silence.

He pushed off the railing like some sort of wild animal about to attack. Addie resisted taking a step back. Barely.

"You want me to *say* something? I just found out I have a kid. A son!" The word came out on a sob. "Me, the kid whose dad couldn't stick around because he loved drinking more than he loved us. Me, who vowed I'd never repeat my childhood… You're telling me that's exactly what I've done, and I didn't even know it!"

*Dear God.* Her breathing shallowed and came in spurts, her whole body simultaneously shaking and overcome with chills. This was what she'd feared ever since their conversation over peanut-butter-and-jelly sandwiches. This was the unbearable pain she'd been afraid of for him. "I'm so sorry." She wanted to cast the blame on her parents. Wanted to somehow prove to Evan that it wasn't her fault. But it was. She'd let it happen. And the aftermath was most certainly on her.

"Stop saying you're sorry," Evan growled.

"I'm sorry."

His hands jutted into the air.

Fine. But what else was she supposed to say? It was the thing that mattered the most. That she meant the most. "Is there anything you want to know?" she asked. *God, let there be something I can say to make this better. Pease, pease, pease.*

Evan rubbed hands over his face. "I want to know how I have a kid and no one told me. And he was adopted without my consent. How is that possible?"

"Honestly, I'm not sure how my parents made that happen. They handled it all. Didn't tell me details. Never asked me what I wanted. I didn't even let myself go there. Didn't let myself believe there were other options, because there weren't for me. I was completely at their mercy with no other way to survive. Dependent on their help. I just did what they told me to. I was so scared, Evan. So, so scared." That fear transferred to the present, causing her limbs to rumble like an earthquake. "I always just assumed they pulled some strings or made it look like we couldn't get in touch with you."

"When of course you could have."

"Yes," she whispered.

"Are they monsters? Who does that to their own child? And to me?"

Addie had considered them exactly that. To this day, she spoke to her parents sparingly. Their relationship had never fully recovered, and she wasn't sure how to even begin walking that trail of forgiveness. Especially when they weren't asking for it. They'd made a huge mistake in not contacting Evan or letting her talk to him. She was just as angry at her parents over how they'd orchestrated things as Evan was.

"I know. You're right, and I can't make excuses for what they did because I don't agree with it. Come back inside. Please. We can talk more. I'll answer any questions you have."

For the faintest of moments, she thought he was going to listen. But then his features hardened, and he let out a sound somewhere near a growl.

"I don't know what questions I have because this possibility didn't exist this morning. How am I supposed to suddenly be able to process?" He hissed the last word.

Maybe Evan was right. Maybe talking wasn't

the best idea. But Addie didn't know what else to do, what else to say. Was there any way to mollify the man when he'd been stunned beyond repair?

"I know you probably hate me right now, and I get that. I deserve that. But please don't leave. We don't have to talk. I just don't want you to leave like this. Or for you to drive while this upset. Just… I can make us some tea or something. We can take a minute and—"

"I don't want tea." His tone bit into her skin, leaving a mark. "I can't even look at you right now."

Ouch.

"I'm not even sure I know who you are. Has everything you've said and done been a lie?"

"Of course not. I'm the same person." *The one who's been falling for you this whole time just like I think you were for me.* Not that Evan was currently going anywhere near those feelings. Had it really just been twenty minutes ago that he'd kissed her like she was the best thing in his world? Like they fit. Like they had a chance.

"I have no idea what to do with all of this." Evan's motion encompassed her, the B & B, maybe even Sawyer, who slept peacefully inside. *Sawyer.* Her son would be brokenhearted if Evan erased himself from their lives. And he had every right to do exactly that. If Addie were in Evan's shoes, she would run as far and fast as she could from someone who'd betrayed her like she had him. "I can't do this." Evan's fingers jerked through his hair, and then he shoved past—careful not to come into contact with her. The porch steps rumbled, and in a matter of seconds, his vehicle was tearing onto the road, engine gunned, tires spitting up gravel.

All of that wondering and praying she'd done regarding how to tell Evan—fearful of how he'd react, fearful of how much the news would wound him.

She didn't have to wonder anymore.

# Chapter Fourteen

Addie had managed to wait all night after Evan left before calling for reinforcements. Her text this morning to Charlie had been cryptic—I really need to talk to someone or I'm going to lose my mind. Charlie had shown up in record time. Addie had filled her new friend in on the sordid details, fearful of being judged, but Charlie had done nothing of the sort.

She'd hugged Addie and prayed with her, and then she'd stayed.

It was equal parts freeing and shame inducing for Addie to admit what she'd allowed to happen and then hadn't figured out a way to correct.

Through the course of the night, Addie had written Evan about twenty texts. Some had been apologies, some explanations and the rest? Crying emojis.

Thankfully she hadn't pressed Send on any of them.

She'd spent the rest of the night baking *pandesal* that Evan would likely never taste in her new-to-her kitchen. The sweet, doughy scent filled the house all the way up to the rafters.

She and Charlie were in the partially-torn-apart second-floor bathroom now, examining the remains of last night's demolition.

"What am I going to do?"

Charlie used her foot to push a fallen mound of tile toward the wall.

"About the guy or the bathroom?"

"Both."

Addie should have told Evan everything *before* he'd started removing tile last night. She could have made the bathroom work when it was still intact. Now she was going to have to figure out how to piece it back together, and just like her personal life, she didn't have any idea how to do that.

Addie covered a yawn. She hadn't even attempted sleeping last night until about four in the morning and then Sawyer had woken up at six. "Do you know anything about tiling a bathroom?" she asked Charlie. The woman could fix a car. In Addie's mind, that made her a superhero who could do anything.

"I don't." Charlie frowned. "Sorry. Wish I did."

Addie's hope crashed.

"But I can ask around. I'm sure there's some-one in town who can help."

For a fee. Addie would never have consid-ered redoing the tile surrounding the tub if Evan hadn't volunteered and insisted.

She deserved as much, Addie knew that, but she also had to figure out what to do. The B & B was still going to open for Old Westbend Week-end, whether Evan was on speaking terms with her or not. Whether she was a horrible person or not. Life would continue to spin.

Sawyer poked his head inside the bathroom door. He'd been running around the second floor, which he considered a racetrack since it circled the stairs.

Charlie engaged in conversation with him, teasing him, making him laugh, giving him some sense of normalcy when Addie felt any-thing but.

They'd become so used to Evan being in their lives. How were they going to adjust to not hear-ing his quiet laugh or seeing that begrudging smile? He'd become her partner in so many ways while working on the B & B. It felt worse than her divorce to know she'd have to figure out how to do life without Evan again, because her marriage had been wrong from the start, but Evan…he'd been right from the start.

What was she going to do with the part of her that had begun falling for him all over again? Addie hadn't processed any of that since Evan's departure. She just…couldn't.

"Stress eating sounds good, doesn't it? And I have enough *pandesal* to feed an army." Not that the man who'd requested it was here to eat any of it.

"I could go for whatever smells so amazing."

Sawyer scampered for the stairs. "Food!"

"That's my kid."

He proceeded to tromp down the steps at a speed that made Addie's nerves screech. At least he was holding on to the railing while he traveled too fast for his little frame.

In the kitchen, Addie made coffee. The house was finally starting to feel complete, especially with the kitchen—the hub of any home—all put back together and in functioning order. Everything felt so clean and crisp. She'd put dishes in the cupboards and set the whole thing up the other night, and the space had since made her happy every time she walked into it.

Would it always make her think of Evan?

Drat. She hadn't considered that part of him helping.

She plated two buns for Sawyer and seated him at the breakfast nook. The coffee finished and she poured mugs for herself and Charlie, plus a covered cup of milk with a straw for Sawyer.

A knock sounded, and then the front door eased partially open. Evan's voice traveled inside. "Everyone decent?"

Addie couldn't have formed words if a million-dollar check was on the line.

"Yep!" Charlie finally answered for her. "We're all good in here."

Evan stepped inside. He'd aged ten years overnight. His eyes were bloodshot, his hair sticking up in so many places and his athletic khakis and T-shirt looked like they'd been dug out of the bottom of a laundry basket.

He was gorgeous.

Addie wanted to cross the space and fall into him. She wanted to wrap her arms around him and tell him how sorry she was. Again. She wanted him to say he understood why it had been so hard for her to tell him. She wanted forgiveness so badly. But most of all, she wanted to dam up his hurt, bottle it and toss it over the mountains so that it could never come back.

His gaze bounced from Addie to Charlie. With only a nod of greeting, he headed up the stairs.

"Gold, frankincense and myrrh." Charlie was reverently shocked. "He's going to work on the bathroom anyway, isn't he?"

By silent agreement, the two of them moved to the base of the stairs and watched the bathroom swallow his form.

Was he? Why would Evan do that? The tears that had finally dried up during the third batch of *pandesal* resurfaced.

"Eban?" Sawyer abandoned his seat and joined them, a half-eaten bun still gripped in his hand.

"He's upstairs. In the bathroom."

Sawyer climbed the steps, Addie shattering with each one. How would Evan react to seeing Sawyer? It would no doubt be painful for him, thinking of their son who he wouldn't get to raise or know.

Chatter filtered down from the bathroom along with Sawyer's giggle.

*He's being good to Sawyer.* Of course, with him showing up here, Addie shouldn't have doubted. But still… Evan didn't owe her or her son anything. After a minute, Sawyer returned to his seat and treat at the breakfast nook, the *pandesal* he'd been carrying now gone.

"Would you look at the time? I should go. I've got…cars to fix. Lots to do. Bill Bronson scheduled an oil change for this morning, and I'd hate to be late. Wouldn't want to keep the mayor from his official duties."

Charlie's continuing string of babble barely

registered with Addie, but once she grabbed her purse and waved goodbye to Sawyer, it all sank in.

"You're leaving me with him? What am I supposed to do? Don't leave me."

"I don't know what to tell you." She winced. "The expertise I have with men is at kindergarten levels."

Charlie hugged her before abandoning her, and then Addie was left with the quiet house, the sounds of Sawyer eating and drinking and the clink-clink coming from the bathroom upstairs.

And dread. She was definitely left with dread.

Addie paced the kitchen for five minutes before plating a couple of the buns. She brought them upstairs along with a mug of coffee, her feet as heavy as boulders. Inside the bathroom, Evan didn't acknowledge her.

She set the items on the bathroom counter. "Thank you, Evan. I don't know what I'd do without your help."

No response. No recognition that he'd even heard her.

Addie retreated to the first floor again to regroup, then worked on fixing the breakfast-nook bench. It had been bothering her all of this time and was one of the last things still unfinished on the main level.

While she worked, Sawyer complained about

missing Belay. Evan had probably left her at home because he hadn't wanted his dog influenced by Addie's evilness.

In between finding activities to occupy Sawyer, Addie dismantled the benches and re-covered and reattached the new yellow vinyl, which she'd gotten at a steep discount.

It brightened the space and left the first floor of the house officially ready for business. The second sounded like it was undergoing a root canal.

Addie had chickened out all morning. No more. She put Sawyer down for his nap despite his protests. Before going upstairs, she stood at the bottom and prayed and sucked in a handful of deep breaths. *Okay, God, I know I don't deserve anything from Evan but anger, but will You help me through this? Help him through this? Amen.*

Upstairs, she found Evan hard at work. Much of the tile was off the wall. He'd filled a big trash can with the discards.

She scanned for something she could do. "Do I need to run to the store and get the new tile? Or did you get it already?"

"It's in my car." Evan didn't look at her when he spoke, but he had uttered words. Addie would take them.

She retrieved the tile, lugging the boxes up

along with the other supplies Evan had brought. She stacked them outside the bathroom, in the hall. Evan had said he'd like to set up a spot to cut the tile upstairs if possible, but that there'd be plenty of dust, so next Addie began taping off an area with tarps to protect the rest of the house. She took out the trash he'd filled and emptied it into the small construction Dumpster outside.

Still nothing from Evan when she returned it empty to the bathroom. "Are you ever going to speak to me again?" She leaned against the bathroom doorframe. "I just need to know how long to plan on enduring this." She toggled a finger between them.

"I haven't decided," Evan said from his crouched position.

"Okay. Take your time. I'll be patient."

"I'm not sure if you can be patient, but I do know you know how to keep a secret."

Addie rubbed a hand over the gaping wound from the bomb Evan had just lobbed, which, interestingly enough, sounded a bit like something an elementary-aged kid would say. "Touché." She swallowed. "You can be mad at me for as long as you want or need. I'm mad at me too. I should have stood up to my parents back then, but honestly, I didn't know what to do. I was such a mess and so young. And you'd just

gone through the amputation. It wasn't a typi-
cal situation. If you hadn't just been through
the accident, I think I would have come to you.
We would have found a way through it. Somehow. But with all that you had going on, I just
didn't know how we'd manage a pregnancy or a
baby. I knew I certainly couldn't. I didn't even
have a part-time job or a hundred bucks to my
name. So opposing my parents' demands..."
Her head shook. It had been impossible. "But all
of that doesn't change the fact that I was wrong.
I should have handled things differently. Especially after I moved out. I'm more sorry than
you'll ever know."

During her speech, Evan had stopped working.

He simply stared at her now, so much pain
etched across his features that it cut her ability
to breathe to asthmatic levels.

Finally, he spoke. "What's he like? Our son?"
His voice cracked on the word *son* and Addie's
whole body trembled.

"He's amazing. Come on. I'll show you."

Evan had spent most of the night lying awake,
angry, confused and hurt beyond anything he'd
ever experienced before.

He hadn't decided what to do about the B &
B until he'd gotten up this morning, and then

he'd known. No matter what Addie had done, he couldn't leave her or the kid in the lurch with guests arriving in mere days. So here he was, remodeling the bathroom while still seething, insides boiling with curiosity about the son he hadn't known existed.

Unfortunately, the woman he'd rather not speak to for the next decade was the only source he had on that. And so, he was stuck.

Addie was waiting for him outside the small bathroom after her *Come on. I'll show you* remark, so Evan abandoned the tile he'd been carefully removing in order to avoid having to redo any backer board and followed her downstairs and into the kitchen.

"Where's Sawyer?"

"Down for his nap."

Without the kid, the house was eerily quiet. Too much room and space for the tension between him and Addie to expand and swallow them whole. He hadn't even brought Belay along today. She'd pouted over that this morning, sitting by the front door, watching his every move. Evan wasn't sure exactly why he'd left her home, but it had felt like keeping a piece of himself detached from Addie and Sawyer. Like he might be present at the B & B, but he wasn't fully there without Belay.

Overnight, Evan had curled into his shell like

a turtle. He'd begun regressing to the old version of himself the minute Addie had broken the news to him. Ever since his mind had been slithering with admonitions—*See? It's better to be on your own. It's better not to even attempt trusting. It's better to be the first one to go.*

The beliefs he'd clung to for so long had been easily resurrected by the woman in front of him.

"Sit." She motioned toward the breakfast nook, which had been repaired.

"This looks good."

"Thanks." She paused, studying him. "I spent the morning doing that since I didn't think you were a big fan of me being in that small bathroom with you."

*You'd be right.* Anger and sadness were wreaking havoc on him, sending his body into the kind of torment he'd endured after losing his leg. And he couldn't even begin to think about Addie herself. How he could go from fearing he loved her to *this* in a matter of seconds.

Addie returned to the table with another plate of *pandesal* and a glass of ice water. He hadn't eaten this morning—hadn't even made coffee before ripping himself out of bed and heading over here with a *the faster he got this done the faster he could escape* mentality. The *pandesal* Addie had brought him upstairs was still on the countertop. He'd managed to resist it by pure determination and righteousness. The coffee hadn't fared the same fate.

It now filled his belly without a companion.

Evan gave in to the temptation of the fresh rolls. They had the slightest hint of sweetness, and Addie served them with raspberry jam. He wolfed them down while she retrieved a laptop and box.

What was in the box?

She waited for him to scoot farther into the bench and then sat next to him. Unexpected. She smelled sweet like the dough. Their arms brushed, and Evan inched away.

She opened the computer and then a file labeled Eli. The first picture hit him like a throat punch. A little boy with his forehead, his eyes, his almost everything stared at the camera with the biggest smile covering his face. His beautiful skin mimicked Addie's but registered a few shades lighter. Another photo showed Eli with two other little boys having a water-balloon fight.

"Those are his little brothers," Addie explained. She clicked on to the next folder, which contained younger photos.

They were going back in time, and each one made it harder and harder to breathe. Evan hadn't realized his cheeks were wet until Addie got up and returned with tissues. Hers were glistening too. He wiped away moisture, blew his nose, then returned to the photos and the information sent by Eli's adoptive parents.

"The only reason I have these is because his parents—his adoptive parents—insisted on an open adoption. They send me updates every year around his birthday." She released a heavy sigh. "It was one thing my parents weren't able to take from me."

Often, they'd included a letter with notes about Eli—a summary of what he was like, who he was becoming, how much they loved him.

*Started walking—ten months.*

*Broke his leg by falling off a swing—six years old.*

*Dotes on his little brothers, making silly faces until they stop crying and start laughing.*

*First crush this year on the neighbor girl. They say they're going to get married someday.*

"He's beautiful." That was the only word Evan could make sense of. To see that vibrant, happy young boy and know that he was his birth father…it inexplicably filled him with pride. What a strange reaction. The baby photos were professionally done and included a shot of Eli's parents staring at him with adoration. Like they'd been given the best gift in the world. *We would have looked at you like that too, little guy. We just wouldn't have had the professional photos. Or the stability. Or a way to provide for you.*

If he and Addie had tried to raise Eli, they would have been doing it without support—at least from her parents. They would have struggled and limped along. They likely would have drowned in bills and worries.

The thought that had plagued Evan all night rose up again. He hadn't been fit to be a father to this boy at the age he'd been. Now? Sure. But then? No way. Addie had been right to place him up for adoption to this family.

She just hadn't been right to not share that information with him.

*You know why she didn't—how her parents threatened her.* She'd certainly explained that part to him in detail. And yet, even with that knowledge, understanding didn't dawn. Forgiveness didn't rise up. Darkness did.

He and Addie could never have provided for Eli what his adoptive parents had. That wasn't an argument Evan would even begin to make. But his upset over not knowing, over how Addie could keep a secret like that for so long…

It killed him. It definitely killed that piece of him that had considered trying to let others in, to not run and protect and shut down this time around.

That option was long gone.

## Chapter Fifteen

Addie took out the trash from the last of the bathroom remodel while stark desperation suffocated her. Two things were currently happening at once. First, the bathroom was about to be finished, and with it, the house officially ready for guests tomorrow. And second, Evan was preparing to leave. Her. Sawyer. Maybe even the town. He hadn't said as much, but she knew.

She knew.

Addie was as certain Evan was leaving as she was of her love for Sawyer. He'd begun the process the night she'd told him about Eli, and he'd been perfecting it ever since.

Upstairs, Sawyer "helped" Evan with the caulking along where the tile met the walls and tub. Addie paused to listen as her son jabbered and Evan inserted a comment at the right spots. He was still being so good to Sawyer. Still treating him well. Still speaking to him. He was still speaking to her, too, when the need arose.

But he was slipping away at the same time.

The relationship that had grown between the two of them during the B & B renovations had *poof*—disappeared. They were like strangers now. Working next to each other at times, but with no more talks, no more touching, no more chance for love. Hard to believe it had only been a couple of days since he'd found out about Eli.

Evan had been pretty quiet on the subject of their son since she'd shown him the pictures and they'd both wept. His distancing of himself had been stealth-like. Too quiet. Like Sawyer when he was playing, and she couldn't hear him. That always ended in trouble.

"We go ice cream?" Sawyer asked, and Addie leaned against the wall in the hallway outside the bathroom to gather her unruly emotions.

"Not this time, squirt." Evan's response held steady, but her pulse did nothing of the sort.

*Tell him the truth—not ever.* She bit her lip to keep the words from coming out.

Thank the good Lord, Sawyer didn't have a clue that Evan was beginning to sever their tie. To her son, Evan looked and talked the same. And he did. But Addie could see the disconnect. The skittish, fearful presence that had taken up residence in the once confident man. She'd done that to him, and it slayed her.

She'd been attempting to hold on to Evan with everything in her. Like a mama tethered to shore, intent on rescuing her child from a riptide current. But he kept slipping through her fingers, drifting further away with each hour.

She was tempted to wreck something in the bathroom or rest of the house just so he'd stay.

But even then, she doubted he would. He was done—with her, with this place.

Before she got caught stalling in the hallway, Addie stepped into the bathroom and continued her cleaning. Evan didn't so much as glance her way, and another chunk of her heart shattered. She'd hoped that somehow he'd find a way to forgive her. That they could finagle a way through this—together this time.

But that hadn't happened despite her incessant prayers. Charlie said that a relationship with God didn't mean that everything would be wonderful all of the time. Just that whether things were good or bad, He was there. That you weren't alone anymore. Addie clung to that now. She might not have experience with God like that yet, but she could trust Charlie to tell her the truth. And she would trust God to walk with her in this mess.

As she'd finished setting up the remaining

bedrooms last night, Addie had concluded that she didn't have anything to lose in continuing to reach out to Evan. Since she'd effectively lost him the night she'd told him about Eli, she only had him to gain. Last time she hadn't been allowed to pursue contact with Evan. This time it would only be fear holding her back. She had to try again, because otherwise she was petrified that when he walked out of this place after the final finishes on the bathroom, she'd never see him again.

And she couldn't handle losing him a second time. Not when there was even the slightest chance she could keep him.

"Sawyer, why don't you run down and get some crackers for a snack?" Addie suggested. "They're in the big cupboard."

Evan wasn't sure if her prompting was about keeping Sawyer fed or about Addie wanting to talk to him alone. Hopefully the first, because he didn't have anything to say to her right now.

"Okay, Mommy!" The little guy scampered off, promising to bring some back for Evan, destroying him slowly.

Ever since he'd found out about Eli, something had shut down inside him. That brokenness he'd feared had risen up, large and in charge and not going away any time soon.

Evan finished the last of the caulking and stepped back to view his work. Not perfect, since he wasn't a master tiler, but good. Certainly better than it had been a few days before. And it was his last project at the B & B. He could finally escape the way these walls had been closing in on him since Addie had told him about Eli. Finally escape the way he wanted to go to her for comfort—comfort he only needed because of the shocking news she'd revealed to him. He still wanted her. And Evan didn't know what to do about that except to run.

She wasn't safe. Trying to make things work with someone who'd proven she couldn't be trusted wouldn't be smart in the least. So he planned to do what Dad had taught him.

And he planned to do it quickly.

"Need some help with that?" Addie motioned to the wall he'd just finished.

He resisted raising an eyebrow at her close proximity. More like he needed her to back off and give him space. "No."

"You sure?"

How did she smell so good while they were working? Evan could guarantee he reeked like a dirty sock. He managed to stay upright, to not lean closer and confirm what his senses were broadcasting.

Addie sat on the closed toilet seat cover. "I miss you, you know."

Evan lowered himself to the edge of the tub and began stacking the last of the supplies. Their knees were close but thankfully not touching. He couldn't handle that right now. In fact, there currently wasn't much on his "could handle" list. "How can you miss me when I'm sitting right here?"

"I miss the guy who was here before you found out about Eli."

"He doesn't exist anymore."

She blinked and pressed her lips tight as if stemming emotion. "I think he does."

"Crackers!" Sawyer marched into the bathroom, proud of his accomplishment. His little palm had about ten crackers, which he divided out between Evan and Addie.

Addie ate the Goldfish he'd brought her. "Yum. Thanks, bugaboo."

Sawyer watched him. "Eban eat." Rather than argue or disappoint the kid, Evan tossed them back.

"Thanks, squirt."

Sawyer beamed. Another portion of Evan died a slow death.

"Can you get us some more?" Addie's request proved that she was sending Sawyer on missions in order to get Evan alone.

Sawyer's head bobbed. "And milk too!"

"No, no, no!" Addie stopped him with a gentle hand to his arm. "We don't need milk. Just crackers."

"Okay, Mommy."

"Phew. That would have been a huge mess."

*I want this.* The thought slammed into Evan with Colorado-gust-of-wind speed. *I want to be part of this. Of them. But I can't.* It was too late. He was too upset. It wouldn't work.

"Evan." Addie leaned forward, her hands landing on his knees. "Tell me that you can never forgive me for what I did."

He swallowed but didn't speak.

"Tell me that you don't feel what I feel. That couldn't have all vanished, could it? There has to be a smidgen of it still alive, doesn't there?"

More than a smidgen.

*I can't tell you any of that. How can I trust you when you didn't tell me about Eli? How can I trust myself to stick around through the hard stuff when all I want to do right now is run?*

"Look at me, Evan." He couldn't seem to obey that command, so her head dipped low, interrupting his line of vision. "I've always wanted to tell you about Eli and didn't know how. I still should have—I'm not denying my mistakes. But ever since you walked back into my life and helped me beyond what any normal human being would do, I've been falling in love with you all over again."

No. She couldn't. It wasn't fair. Not after what Evan had wanted, had hoped he might be able to pursue with her—if he could have managed to commit and stay.

"It's okay if you never say it back to me. That doesn't change the fact that I gave you my heart a long time ago, and I don't think it's ever going to return to me." Her features softened, going from fighter to peacemaker. "And I'm okay with that. As long as you know that I'm here. That if you can ever forgive me, I'll be waiting for you. And if you can't…" Moisture filled those eyes that owned him. "Then you can't. And there's nothing I can do to make you." That realization scrawled across her face, and yet, somehow, she still looked as if she would be okay no matter what. As if she had Someone filling her with peace.

Evan was jealous. He was the one who'd had a strong relationship with God at the start of all this. But now Addie was like an anchor, and he was the drifting trash bag getting tossed around on the waves.

Maybe he could find a way to forgive Addie, but could he find a way to trust and stay? Because the moment things had gone wrong, his whole instinct had been to retreat. And that scared him more than anything.

"I have to go. I need space."

"Are you ever coming back?"

"I don't know." He stood, and Addie rose with him. Her arms wrapped around his middle, her ear pressed against his chest, surely taking in his thundering heartbeats. Evan didn't hold her back. He couldn't. Just as he was about to disentangle himself from her, Sawyer barreled into the bathroom, the crackers in his fist dropping to the floor and then crunching under his feet like he was a baby Godzilla as he rushed to join their awkward embrace. His little arms looped around their legs, and his cheek landed against Evan's thigh. *Really, God? I'm barely holding myself together right now. Are You sending the kid in here to topple me over? Where are You in all of this?* Evan couldn't sort it out.

Addie's arms finally dropped away. Remorse flared at the loss of her. She scooped up Sawyer, replacing him. Good. At least the two of them had each other. When Evan broke out of here, he'd be on his own again. That was what he'd planned on when rolling into town. He just hadn't expected it to be such a disappointment.

"Bye, squirt." Evan ruffled Sawyer's hair with his palm, the movement filling Addie with sorrow.

He held her gaze but didn't speak. And then he was gone.

"Mommy, I want milk."

"Okay, bug." Addie swallowed a wave of sorrow, willing herself not to scream or kick a hole in the wall or chase after Evan. She had to let him go. "We'll get you some milk. Just let me clean this up first." She set Sawyer down, and her hand shook as she wiped up the remnants of the crackers Sawyer had just dropped in his haste to get in on a hug—a one-sided embrace Evan hadn't participated in.

Addie wanted to lay her cheek on the cool tile floor and never get up. She wanted to cancel the reservations for tomorrow, then head back in time and decide not to move to Westbend. Not to try to open the B & B on her own, thereby requiring so much help that The Best Guy in the World had to step in to rescue her.

She wanted Evan to forgive her. She wanted him to love her back.

"I get the milk, Mommy." Sawyer took off before she could catch him, and Addie winced.

"Just wait and I'll pour it for you!"

Sawyer either didn't hear her or chose not to. It was a toss-up. Addie quickly finished collecting the last of the supplies that still littered the bathroom. The ones Evan had begun stacking. She gathered everything and then stepped to the doorway, scanning the space for anything left behind.

It looked really good. So much better than it had before the tile redo. The floor tile was still older, but she had a rug to cover and brighten it. She nudged the light off with her elbow and walked into the kitchen in time to see Sawyer attempting—and failing miserably—to fill his cup with milk. He'd set it on the floor, which should have helped, but the carton was full and therefore hard to get the right angle with.

"Oh-oh. I spilleded." Sawyer gave it another go. Another round of milk missed the cup. "I clean it up, Mommy." He raced for the paper towels, which were on the counter, managing to yank the whole roll down. They stretched across the kitchen as he hurried back to the mess he'd made.

Addie sat down on the floor next to the spilled milk, took the paper towels from him and began sopping it up. She didn't trust herself to speak right now. She was afraid she'd take out the situation with Evan on her son, and she *really* didn't want to do that. Sawyer was innocent in all of this. And he was the best thing in her world.

"Eban bye-bye?"

And she'd been doing so well. "Yes, honey. Evan went bye-bye." Probably forever. Ugh! Why'd she have to go and fall for him all over again? But really, how could she *not* love a man like that? Evan was everything Addie wanted in a partner. Completely sacrificial. He'd cared for Sawyer; that much was obvious. And even when he was upset with her, he still showed up to help. That could have been about him wanting to know more about Eli, but Addie didn't think so. If that were the case, he'd have banged on the door and demanded as much. He was too good to leave her hanging.

Too good for her, period.

Would he show up for his Old Westbend Weekend hero role on Saturday? The man definitely fit the bill. But Addie wanted him to be her own personal hero. Not the town's. She wanted him to herself for the next handful of decades. And she definitely didn't deserve that.

She wasn't even going to hope for that.

Today was goodbye, and she *had* to wrap her brain around that blatant truth.

"Mommy okay?" Sawyer hunched over enough to peer into her face, his hands on his knees...standing right in the middle of the remaining milk. *You've got to be kidding me.* Addie half laughed, half moaned, because it was either that or cry yet again.

"Yeah." She caught him, squeezing him tight, wiping off his feet with a paper towel. She smooched his soft cheeks, creating silly noises that made him laugh. "Mommy's going to be okay."

Somehow. She had to figure out a way, because she had a little boy to raise who needed his mama. And she wasn't about to fail him too.

## Chapter Sixteen

"This is not my idea of a good time. Why'd I let you talk me into this again?" Jace tromped behind Evan on the trail as the sun slid behind the mountains.

Before all of the light disappeared, they needed to find a spot to camp out for the night, and Evan had just spied something that would work. A cove that would allow for a fire, with boulders on one side and Evergreens flanking behind.

Perfect.

The temperature had been in the low sixties, but it would drop now, which was why they had thermal sleeping bags strapped to their backs.

"We both know I didn't invite you on this little excursion," he answered his brother. "I notified you that I was going because that's the proper protocol. You're the one who insisted on inviting yourself along." Evan would have preferred escaping alone, but he hadn't been sure how to tell his brother that without completely offending him. Even for guys, that would have been harsh. He'd wanted to get away from everything, so once he'd left Addie's earlier today, he'd thrown supplies into a backpack. Enough to last him for an extended hike.

He'd planned to spend the night outside—just him and the vast universe. Now because his brother had tagged along, it was just him, the universe and Jace.

They reached the spot and set up quickly, starting a controlled fire stationed between them and the boulder. After eating the sandwiches they'd packed, Evan removed his prosthesis, cared for his limb and then stretched out in his bag. He was out of shape from the few weeks without hiking or climbing, and his body felt the strain. It was a welcome exhaustion though. If he could succumb to it, then he wouldn't have to think about how crushing the last few days had been or delve into how he could be angry with Addie and miss her at the same time.

"There are rocks biting into my back. I could be in bed with my wife right now." Jace gave an exaggerated huff and settled his arms behind his head after adjusting his bag around him. If Evan wasn't mistaken, a half grin climbed his face.

"You're a whiner, you know that?"

A chuckle answered.

"Don't you have studying to be doing?" Evan poked. It seemed the brotherly thing to do.

"I'm allowed to take a short break to spend some quality time with my brother, who's always traveling and never visits. You really are introverted, aren't you? Can't spend more than a minute with anyone but Addie. You were with her nonstop for a couple weeks. What's up with that? I think I'm offended."

"It wasn't nonstop. I finished up some projects at Mom's along the way." But he'd definitely spent major chunks of time with Addie. Time spent talking and getting to know each other again. Time spent falling for her. Time she didn't use to tell him about Eli.

"Next you're going to tell me she's prettier than me," Jace poked back, because of course Evan had told him everything, and his brother couldn't leave well enough alone.

"She is." Addie was the kind of beautiful a man could appreciate for the rest of his life. If Evan were capable of being that kind of man. What did it say about him that he'd run? Exactly what he'd been afraid he would do the whole time. He'd left not only Addie, but Sawyer. And the kid didn't deserve that. He didn't know what had transpired between his adults. He just deserved to be loved. "I'm guessing Mackenzie sent you along to make me process all of the stuff with Addie."

"Nah." Jace tossed a pebble about ten yards, and it skittered into the bushes. "Kenzie's not that way. She tends to stay out of people's love business. Too messy for her."

*Love business.* Funny name for something that didn't exist. "Could you love someone who'd kept something like that from you?"

The fire crackled. *Pop-pop.* Evan watched the spark land and made sure it faded to nonexistent. Some seasons fires weren't even allowed, but there'd been enough moisture this spring that no restrictions had been put in place yet this year.

"It depends, I guess, on whether they're worth working through something like that."

Addie thought she'd made so many mistakes in life that she could never start over. Start fresh. She'd told Evan as much during their time working on the B & B. Evan didn't believe anyone was past a restart, but he wasn't sure if he could just forget everything that had transpired between them.

After they'd looked through Eli's pictures the other day, Addie had given him a box filled with letters that she'd written him every year on Eli's birthday. He'd finally read them after leaving the B & B today. They'd been dripping with remorse. They'd shown him how much she'd thought about their son—and him—over the years. They were heartbreaking and terribly hard to read, and at the same time had helped him understand so much of what Addie had gone through.

Evan was beginning to grasp how things had unfolded. How she'd been trapped and then hadn't known how to get herself out of the predicament. Telling him about Eli would never have been easy at any point, but calling him out of the blue to share that news would have been *hard*. And then when they'd been working on the B & B and Evan had brought up Luc Wilder and his daughter…his upset over that scenario would have made sharing the truth with him that much more impossible.

"Last summer when I first got to Wilder Ranch, I didn't let anyone—including Kenzie—know about my concussion right away. And it wasn't necessarily because I wanted to hide anything. I just…wasn't ready to deal with it myself. Informing other people meant accepting it. Maybe Addie just didn't know how to deal. If her parents did what she said they did—threatening her even—then she basically went through a trauma of her own. She probably didn't know how to get out of that lie after the fact."

Her own trauma. Evan hadn't thought of it that way before. Addie must have felt completely abandoned during that time. He'd been a tenth of himself. Her parents had been threatening her like Jace said. Evan believed her on that. They'd been strict from the start.

"That actually makes sense."

"I do that a lot," Jace quipped.

"Not really." Evan's mouth hitched in the silence. It was good to have a brother to spar with. *And that's exactly what Eli has.* Two little brothers, in fact. Those pictures had been...they'd been a relief. Evan may not have been involved in that decision at the time, but he couldn't deny God had protected Eli and brought him to exactly where he was supposed to be.

It was depressing to think that he would have stunk at being a father at that age, but he'd been barely eighteen and recovering from his accident.

"I always thought Dad basically abandoned us. And that's been my biggest struggle with Eli. That I did the same to him and I didn't even have a choice in the matter."

"Dad had a disease, E. If he'd been in his right mind, I doubt he would have chosen that."

"I forget that alcoholism is referred to as a disease. As a kid, watching him, it didn't feel that way."

"Nope. As a kid it felt...personal. One of the guys I competed with—alcoholism ran in his family, and he suffered from it too. He talked about how it was an obsession. How it was all he thought about, but at the same time, he didn't even realize it was consuming him. He said it wasn't even a want. Felt like a need. A desperate one. It changes the brain so that the only thing that will fill the desire is more alcohol. He'd been sober for six months at the time. It helped me understand better, because he was a good guy. Made me realize that underneath the disease, Dad was probably a good guy too. I would guess that's why Mom married him."

Emotion built behind Evan's eyes, blurring the stars that had begun to peek through the black sheet of sky. How had he never thought about Dad that way? The truth was, he'd never wanted to learn. Never wanted to delve into the whys. He'd just lived in the left behinds.

And Evan had been letting their dad control who he was for a long, long time.

Jace's phone chirped, and he scrambled to get it out of his pocket. "Reception!" His fingers flew over the keys.

Evan tossed a handful of pebbles at Jace. "Tell Mackenzie hi for me, you schmoopy schmoop."

Jace was too distracted by the text conversation to pay any attention to Evan. He sported a dopey smile over something she'd said.

"And tell her she's welcome to demand you come home. Tell her you're whipped and—"

"I can hear you, you know. And don't try to send me away. Pretty sure I'm the best thing you've got out here in the middle of nowhere. You think nature would have given you as good of answers as I did tonight? I don't think so." Jace smirked and turned his attention back to his phone.

Evan shook his head, a grin reaching for existence. His brother was right—he was glad he was here *and* glad for the wisdom dump Jace had just unloaded.

But no way did Evan plan to admit any of that.

Turns out, Addie's "okay" was the wobbly kind of okay. By Saturday morning, she'd managed a semblance of normalcy. On the outside, she was functioning. Internally, not so much. Charlie had been checking in on her with a constant string of supportive texts since Evan's departure on Thursday. Addie was eternally grateful for the other woman. Without her prayers, she wasn't sure she'd be surviving right now.

On a scale of one to ten, she missed Evan at a twenty. Sawyer missed him—and Belay—at fifteen each. That brought them to fifty between the two of them. If she were gauging their response to Evan's departure as a disaster, they'd be calling in the National Guard right now.

"Dear, do you have any hot tea?" Mrs. Pepski entered the kitchen where Addie was plating the last of the warm chocolate-chip muffins. She'd made blueberry earlier, but with two elementary-aged girls staying at the B & B with their parents, she'd wanted something even more kid friendly. Something to make their parents leave a five-star review and come back to stay again.

Chocolate was always a good idea.

"Of course. It's right out on the coffee bar. Let me show you." When the Pepskis had arrived yesterday, Addie had helped them lug suitcases up to their room. She'd been slightly afraid that they'd see the stairs and declare they had to find somewhere else to stay, but the elderly couple had been quite spry, jokingly telling her that stairs kept them young and Mr. Pepski's artificial hips in working condition.

Everyone who'd stayed last night had been really great guests. Addie could only hope it was a prediction of things to come. "Here you go." She lifted an empty mug from the stack. "May I?"

At Mrs. Pepski's nod, Addie filled her cup

with hot water and showed her the tea options. The woman finished the rest herself, and Addie delivered the warm muffins to the breakfast cart.

"Those smell so good!" One of the Balter girls came over and peered inside the cloth napkin covering the muffins. "Chocolate!" She snagged one without a plate, which made her mom yelp.

Addie waved away the mom's concern. "They're kids. Let them be kids."

"Are you going to watch us in the parade this morning, Ms. Addie?"

"Just Addie is fine, and yes, I am." In fact, she had about five minutes to get out the door and go set up the B & B table before the weekend officially started.

After confirming that all of the guests had her cell number if they had any issues, she rushed into her room and threw on some makeup. Her hair was freshly washed, so she left it straight and long. It was strange, after weeks of remodeling and wearing work clothes, to actually dress to be seen in public. Still, Old Westbend Weekend was a relaxed affair, so she went with boyfriend jeans, a navy top and a pair of flats. Casual and yet still professional enough to say business owner. *I can't believe I am that!* If not for Evan and Charlie and God, she wouldn't be. Her best-laid plans would have collapsed without all of them swooping in and coming through. What must people have thought of her for taking the risk she had? It was only by the grace of God the B & B had gotten done in time and hadn't folded financially during the process.

Despite her many mistakes in life and the most recent ones with Evan, Addie felt God *with* her. Evan might have taken off, but God hadn't. She was starting to understand that His love had nothing to do with her actions. She was starting to understand what had been missing in her life before forging a relationship with Him. Even if she and Evan never spoke to each other again, Addie wasn't alone. She had a good Father now.

Armed with the bag of supplies she'd set out last night, Addie scooped up Sawyer from where he was playing with cars at the breakfast nook and the two of them drove the couple of blocks to town. Addie would normally take the time to walk in a situation like this because parking would be a bear today, but she had too many supplies for the B & B table. A sign would be provided by the city due to her sponsorship, but she'd also printed brochures, pens, stress balls and a few other novelty items to hand out. Along with a sheet for newsletter sign-ups for specials and deals for the B & B. That had been coached by Charlie, of course. Bless her.

She passed Alma's house as she looked for a parking spot. The woman had her "food truck" out front, and judging by the small white bags people carried and the sweet, sugary smell wafting in Addie's open car window, she was selling fresh mini donuts. From the looks of the line, she was raking in the dough. *Good for you, Alma.*

By the time Addie got things situated, the sidewalks were already streaming with people. Addie was stationed near the grassy area by the city hall building, an older brick structure which had been added to the national historical registry. A covered stage, which would host bands and performances throughout the day, stood in front.

The first thing on the schedule of events was Evan. Ahem. The first thing on the schedule of events was honoring the Westbend hometown heroes. The ceremony would kick things off before the parade.

*If* Evan was still in town and showed up today, Addie would see him. At least from a distance. *God, whatever happens today—whether I get to talk to Evan or not—will You be with both of us?* Addie hated the idea of seeing Evan from afar and knowing he didn't want to speak to her. It hurt thinking about it. Experiencing it would be pure torment.

"I wanna cookie, Mommy." Sawyer pushed around the brochures she had just laid out until they were a hodgepodge mess.

"I don't have a cookie for you, bugaboo. You just had a chocolate-chip muffin before we left the house."

"But I want a cookie!" He crossed his arms and his lower lip wobbled. Oh boy. Could he pick a worse time or place for a tantrum?

"I have a granola bar in my bag." Addie began digging for it, finding a pen, a toy car, a small book—

"No! I wanna cookie!" The words escalated to screeching levels, and the woman who ran the quilting store paused from setting up her table to give Addie one of those *why don't you control your kid* looks.

*Trust me, lady, I'm working on it.*

"There's my tiny troublemaker." Addie turned to see Charlie scooping up Sawyer. "Hey, little man."

"Hi-hi!" Sawyer brightened and immediately dropped the crying act. He loved attention from anyone, but Charlie was quickly shooting to the top of his list of favorite people. Probably because she usually had a treat or something to distract him in her pocket.

She held out a fidget spinner. "Check this

out. Someone left it at the shop and didn't come back to claim it."

Sawyer babbled about the toy, quickly sending the small gear flying and the bright green whirling.

"You're a child whisperer." Addie sucked in a relieved breath. She'd been off her mom game the last few days. She'd been off any and all of the games the last few days. The stress from losing Evan again had a way of making even the smallest tasks feel impossible. "Thank you."

Charlie's relaxed smile shot a pinch of jealousy through Addie. She'd get back to that place again someday, right?

"You're welcome. Listen, my brother is in town. He's going to help me man the garage's table today, so I can take Sawyer over to the parade and stake out a spot if you want. You can join us when you get a break over here."

"That would be fantastic. I was just contemplating how I was going to keep him entertained if anyone wanted to ask questions about the B & B. I hadn't really thought that through." Her mind definitely hadn't been functioning at its best this week. Not with all of the Eli-Evan stress.

"You want to go see the parade?" Charlie checked with Sawyer, who punched a fist into the air.

"Pease!"

They laughed, and Addie waved as the two of them bounded through the crowd, Charlie pretending to drop Sawyer every few steps, causing his giggle to echo back to Addie.

"Ladies and gentlemen." Bill Bronson used the microphone to greet the crowd, chest puffed at being front and center. "We're so glad you're here. Happy Old Westbend Weekend!" A smattering of people whooped or clapped. If Evan were next to her, they'd no doubt be sharing a laugh over Bill's love for the spotlight. Would she ever find someone who got her like Evan did? Who found the same things funny and the same things important? Who she was attracted to? Who she liked spending time with?

*You're growing a substantial list there, girl.* And the lengthier the list, the more depressing the thought that she'd forever wounded the one guy she was crazy about, and it was going to be a long, lonely life without him.

# Chapter Seventeen

Bill spoke for six minutes about the town's history. Sure, that was the focus of the weekend, but Addie barely resisted jumping on stage to muzzle him. *Move it along, Bronson.* Was Evan here or not? Her patience had evaporated.

"We're kicking off the weekend by honoring the next generation of hometown heroes."

*Finally!*

"I'd like to welcome hometown hero Evan Hawke to the stage. He's an overcomer who's devoted his life to helping victims of trauma, and we couldn't be prouder to call him one of our own."

Addie held her breath, completely expecting a moment like in *The Sound of Music* when the von Trapp family was called for repeatedly before everyone realized they'd escaped.

But that didn't happen. Evan walked onstage

and took his place next to Bill, and so much relief filled her that her audible sigh made the quilting store owner glance her way again.

Oops.

He was dressed in a short-sleeved button-down and khaki shorts. Had his hair gotten longer in the last day and a half? He'd gained a pink hue to his complexion, and the restless agitation that had controlled his features when he'd left the B & B was gone, replaced by something calmer.

*Thank You, God, for whatever put that there.*

She'd been so afraid that he wouldn't show. She was so relieved to see him, to know he was okay, even if he wasn't hers.

*God, if this is the answer to my prayers, I'll take it.*

Bill continued. "Evan is going to hand out the plaques of recognition while I tell you a little about each of the kids being honored today."

Evan shifted uncomfortably much like he'd done in her kitchen that first day he'd stopped by the B & B. The shy factor was in full force, and he didn't scan the crowd. Just kept focused on the master of ceremonies as if doing anything out of the script would cause him to turn to dust. Evan probably didn't want to be anywhere near here, between the stage, the crowd and her, but he'd shown up.

He had a habit of doing that.

Bill read from a sheet in his hand about each of the kids, and they came on stage when he called their names. They ranged in age from sixteen to four, and each had overcome something in their lives or made a difference in their community. The little boy—like Evan had told her—had been born with only one arm and had started a charity to send kids to camp with other children who'd lost a limb or been born without.

Evan handed out the plaques and either shook their hands or bumped fists. After all of that worrying he did about being in front of a crowd, he was a natural. No tripping. No dropping a plaque. Was there anything he couldn't do?

*Forgive me. Love me.*

Well. That was a terrible internal response to a rhetorical question.

After the last kid received their award, Evan scanned the crowd. Addie's breath jumbled in her throat when his gaze landed on her and stuck like Sawyer's head through the porch spindles.

And then Evan did the strangest thing. He stepped forward, next to Bill Bronson, and motioned that he wanted to use the microphone. For a second Addie thought there was going to be a struggle over the thing. Bill covered the top and spoke to Evan. After some words exchanged back and forth, the mayor reluctantly handed the mic over, acting like he'd just lost his best friend.

And then Evan Hawke—the man who claimed to loathe the spotlight—stepped directly into it.

Evan's heart was beating way too fast. Much more and he'd find himself in a puddle on the stage instead of standing. The microphone he'd wrestled away from Bill burned his palm and almost slipped through his grasp from the sweat flooding his body.

He cleared his throat, buying time. "I just wanted to say congratulations to these kids. They're the true heroes, and it's an honor to stand here next to them." *Okay, that wasn't so bad. Now what?*

He wasn't sure what he was doing or thinking. He certainly hadn't planned to steal the mic from Bill Bronson. But when he'd looked out into the crowd and found Addie gazing back at him, her lips bowed in greeting, her eyes shouting that they believed in him, he'd known without a doubt that no matter what had happened between them in the past or whatever happened in the future, he couldn't live without her.

The next thing he knew, he'd taken over the stage. Now the crowd watched him expectantly, but he couldn't think over the roaring and pounding of his pulse.

Addie's fingertips covered her mouth as she stared raptly at him.

"I never expected to receive such a warm welcome when I returned to town. The place I grew up and lost part of myself." He glanced down at his leg. He'd worn shorts today so that he could shout who he was loud and proud—especially with these amazing kids watching him. "And then found myself again. This town..." *Great.* He was going to get emotional. "Supported my family many times over the years." When Dad had passed away. After his accident. And more recently when his mom had been sick. "And I just wanted you to know how much I appreciate that and what it means to me." He'd been scanning the crowd but now zeroed in on Addie. "To belong." *If you'll still have me.*

His limbs went numb. Ho-boy. The stage-fright part was kicking in now. There were so many things he wanted to say to Addie. So many things he'd figured out while camping with Jace.

The microphone was ripped from his grip. "Thank you, Evan." Bill's voice boomed from the speakers. He then launched into announcements about the day's schedule as Evan and the kids filed off the stage.

He reached the side, and numerous people greeted him, thanking him. It felt almost wrong considering how much Evan loved doing what he did.

Bill announced that the parade was about to start, and the crowd began dispersing. Once people parted, Evan made his way toward the back where Addie's table was. He hurried, hoping that she wouldn't take off to watch the parade with Sawyer before he could catch her.

When he neared her table, she was talking to a patron who was asking questions. He stayed out of her line of sight, behind a group of people, listening as she shared about the different rooms and amenities Little Red Hen Bed & Breakfast offered. He was proud of her for reopening the B & B and making her dreams happen. Proud of her for raising Sawyer like a champ…and proud of her for overcoming the terrible mess that had gone down with her parents and Eli. She'd managed a healthy pregnancy throughout all of that, had brought a beautiful boy into the world. Addie had done her very best with the situation she'd been handed.

Evan could see that now.

He could see so many things now.

Everything he'd talked about with Jace had freed him in ways he'd never expected to experience. Dad hadn't chosen to abandon them.

He'd been sick. Evan didn't have to follow in his footsteps anymore. He could choose differently. He could choose to trust God that he hadn't abandoned Eli. He could fight that theory back with a stick, knowing it wasn't true. Asking God to help him believe it with all of himself. And he could finally leave behind his run-first, don't-get-hurt theory.

He'd never wanted to let go of anything more.

Inviting and keeping people in his life would be a lot easier now that he could bury the dread that he'd repeat the past. Even kids were an option now. He thought of Sawyer.

Definitely an option.

Evan had accused Addie of not being truthful about more than Eli, but that had come from a place of wounding. In his gut, he was confident in who she was and that she'd told him everything. Rebuilding trust between them might take some time, but Evan was game.

He was game for a lot of things he'd recently been afraid to pursue.

Once the patron walked away, Evan approached the front of the table. Addie was straightening brochures. When she looked up and saw him, she froze.

How was it possible to have missed her in the short time he'd been gone? Evan had gone soft. He'd turned into his schmoopy brother.

Strangely enough, he was okay with that, though Jace was going to have a field day with this new development.

"I'm sorry I ran. I have a thing with that. Or at least I used to."

Her eyebrows shot up. "Used to?"

"That's what I hope."

She picked up a stress ball that had the B & B information on it and squeezed. "I'm just glad you're okay and that you're back. And that you're speaking to me." *Squeeze. Squeeze.* "I heard through the grapevine that your mom's house sold. I know the couple from church. They're pregnant and super sweet. It will be a good fit for them." *Squeeze. Squeeze.*

She was babbling. And her eyes seemed to be asking him if his mom's house was the reason he hadn't left town yet.

It wasn't.

*Squeeze. Squeeze.*

"Addie." He reached across and stilled her hand before rounding the table so that he could be closer to her. Almost everyone had moved over to the parade now, and anyone left behind was busy prepping the stage and not paying any attention to them.

"We have some things to work through, but…" When her fingers scuttled through her hair, strawberries and cream wafted his way. "I understand why you did what you did and how things spiraled so out of control. And I want to stop running and stay. With you. And Sawyer."

Belonging and choosing to stay? Those were new for him. Choosing not to let his dad's *disease* dictate his actions and decisions? Also new for him.

But they felt like really, really good ideas. Evan would even go so far as to say his mom would approve. Forgiving and pursuing and loving Addie would be his mom's favorite idea of his yet.

*What?* Addie reeled from what Evan had just declared. He wanted to stay with her and Sawyer? But how could he choose her after what she'd kept from him? And should he?

"Evan, what if I'm not good enough for you? What if you *should* run this time? After everything with Eli, I don't deserve—"

"Hush, now. It doesn't matter what you think."

"What?" She laughed, ending on a moan. "But you can't…" *Love me.*

"Actually, I can." His hands framed her cheeks. "I can love you. And I do." Her legs forgot how to work for a second, her knees swirling. There was no doubt, no coercion in his expression. "I loved you then too. I just…don't say the words that often."

"I knew it then." Her lungs filled with the sweetest air. "But the words aren't so bad." Her cheeks creased. Actions were even better, and that was an area Evan excelled at. "I love you too, Evan."

Relief and happiness lit up his face, turning his features to stunning and distracting and yum.

"I realized something while I was stomping out my frustrations and sleeping under the stars. And listening to my brother, who should be some kind of relationship doctor, but don't you dare tell him I said that." Evan's amusement caused her middle to tighten. "If I can still love you when you weren't able to tell me about Eli long ago, or even when we ran into each other in town or worked on the B & B, then you can love me even when I'm broken. Even when I make mistakes. Even when I'm afraid I'm not enough or don't know how to do a relationship well. That I'm going to mess it all up."

*He loves me. He's choosing me despite our past, despite my mistakes.* Addie let that knowledge sink in, let it wash over her. "I'd love you through anything, Evan Hawke. You don't have to be perfect or have it all together. Not for me. I want you just as you are." If he was broken, then he was the best bit of broken she'd ever encountered.

A wince turned his expression serious. "Addie...you should probably know that I called your parents."

Her jaw dropped at his admission. "What? How? Why?"

"I found their information online. I had to talk to them. I apologized for my part in what happened."

Only Evan would take that step when so, so much of the blame rested solely on her parents. This was what drew her to him. He'd claimed that Luc Wilder was a better man than he was, but that was nowhere near the truth. Evan Hawke was the best of the best—dependable and oozing with goodness, beyond trustworthy, and more forgiving than even he believed himself to be.

"What did they say?"

"They apologized too."

Relief Addie hadn't even known she craved crashed through her.

"It doesn't mean everything is perfect. Obviously, there's a lot to process there, but it was still good to clear the air. I think they have more regrets than you know. And that maybe, like you, they weren't sure how to voice them."

Addie had been angry at her parents for so many years. The idea of taking steps to mend that relationship rekindled a long-buried hope.

Maybe she and Evan could move in that direction together…slowly. Carefully.

Moisture christened Addie's cheeks, notifying her that she was crying yet again. "I don't deserve you, Evan. Or your forgiveness. Or your love."

"Too late. You already have it." He concentrated on performing windshield-wiper duties for her face. "You're going to need to slow the waterworks down, honey. I can't keep up."

She laughed and hiccupped. "I've never cried so much in my whole life. And if anyone is broken, it's me. Not you."

"We can fight about that later." His smile made her stomach do somersaults. So did the fact that he was zeroing in on her lips.

She gave his shirt a tug on the way down so that his mouth would reach hers faster. Evan tasted like home. Like they could belong to each other and with each other and would do whatever it took to make things work. Was there anything better than that?

The kiss wasn't nearly long enough, but since they were standing in the town square, Addie didn't complain *too* much when Evan eased back. "Addie Ricci." His fingers threaded through hers and squeezed. "Will you be my girlfriend?"

She laughed, delight sparking. It was the

same thing he'd asked her that summer. Only he'd been so nervous then, studying the dash and steering wheel of his beater car. Looking anywhere but at her.

Addie wanted exactly what Evan was offering—a chance to start over, to let their love grow a second time, to fight for a future she'd only dreamed about.

"Yes." Definitely yes. "What about your schedule? And your work?"

"We'll figure it out." His hands moved to her shoulders, kneading the muscles that stretched up her neck, turning her to liquid. "I'll get home between trips to see you two." He'd called Westbend *home* and included Sawyer. *Be still my heart.* Relief and bliss and anticipation fired from every nerve ending in her body. "And then when we do our fall schedule, Christopher and I are planning to relocate everything to Colorado. His wife wants to be near her parents in Denver, and I have a new vested interest in staying close." Evan's eyes were warm and soft. "We'll still travel but within the state. It won't be nearly as far, and the trips won't be as long."

"You're going to live in Westbend when you're not traveling." Addie said it with wonder, letting it sink in, letting herself believe in a future she'd so recently thought impossible.

"Yes, but more important, I'm going to come home to you between trips. Always."

*Always.* Her heart expanded. "What else did you cook up in the short time you were gone?"

His voice hitched low. "Kissing you. Definitely kissing you."

"I approve of that option. What else you got?"

"Ah-ah-ah." His head shook, teasing. "I'm not sure you're ready for the rest of it right now, so you're going to have to wait and see."

She'd been waiting for him for ten years. She could manage a few more months. But not *that* much more.

"But just to give you a hint, it involves never leaving you and Sawyer."

She slid hands behind his neck, angling him down for another kiss just because she could.

Because he was her *boyfriend.* The word made her mouth curve while they were still lip-locked.

"Mommy kiss! Mommy kiss!" Sawyer's squawk interrupted them, and Addie and Evan jumped apart.

"Sorry!" Charlie called out, amusement weighing down the apology. "Little guy wanted his mama, so we headed over to find you. Thought you'd be *working*."

They laughed and Sawyer cheered, "Eban, Eban, Eban!"

Evan caught him when he lunged. "Hey, squirt. I missed you."

Sawyer curled arms around Evan's neck in a hug and held on. Addie straight up refused to cry again, though her emotions were breaking through the ceiling of the all-the-feels chart.

"The collector cars are next in the parade," Charlie piped up. "And I can't *bear* to miss those, so I'm out of here. Do try not to miss me though." Her laughter floated back to them as she scurried away as if smells-like-fish Pete Deller was on her tail.

"What do you think? Should we catch the rest of the parade?" Evan asked. "Everyone is over there, so you can probably leave the B & B table unmanned for a bit."

"Let's do it."

Evan swung Sawyer up on his shoulders, and he clung to Evan's hair in panic. "No-no-no."

"Here." Evan caught his hands, steadying him. "You're good. I've got you. I'm not going to let anything happen to you."

*I'm not going to let anything happen to you.* Addie let that promise to her son sink in, knowing that Evan meant it as far more than this minute or even this day. And that was more than she could have ever hoped for. It was one thing for her to fall in love, but it was a whole other thing for Evan to feel the way he did about Sawyer.

To know that Evan would be there for Sawyer no matter what. To know that he was choosing not only her, but her son.

Both of them.

Because someday, if Eli ever wanted answers from them, if he ever wanted to meet them, they could do it together. They could assure him of how much they'd loved him and explain that they'd been too young to raise him. They'd been babies themselves. They'd been incapable of providing the life and family he deserved. None of the other drama mattered.

Once Evan made sure Sawyer was comfortable and felt safe, he reached for her hand. The three of them walked over to the parade, but for Addie, it was far more than that.

They were walking into the future, and for once, it felt like exactly where she was supposed to be.

# *Epilogue*

Evan wasn't supposed to be home until tomorrow, but when the group had finished their climb in Yosemite earlier today, he'd been unable to resist catching an earlier flight. This had been his and Christopher's last summer expedition. From now on, their trips were all scheduled in Colorado. During the winter, Evan would have some down weeks, and he knew exactly what he wanted to do with those.

It was ten o'clock by the time he arrived at the B & B. Addie and Sawyer had recently moved into the cottage out back. He'd helped her get it livable, and she'd started renting out the small room behind the kitchen for extra income. He usually stayed there when he was in town. It was nice to be close to her and Sawyer since their time together was often limited.

He parked and walked around the B & B to

Addie's front door. Lights were still on, so she must be up. Evan knocked lightly.

The door flew open as Addie let out a squeal. "You're back early." She landed against him in a heap, her arms flung around him.

Evan breathed in her sweetness, burying his nose in her neck. "I missed you a crazy, pathetic amount."

She laughed. "Me too!" She cradled his face and kissed him, and he sank into her, into being home. Since they'd first committed to each other again, Evan had wanted to give the two of them time to make sure they worked and made sense. He hadn't wanted to rush things. But the last few months had just proven that they were right for each other. Every chance he could he'd been in Westbend. And when he'd been gone on trips, he'd been as schmoopy as his brother, hoping for reception so that he could hear from Addie, talk to Addie, text Addie. He'd been running to her instead of from her, and not only did it feel right, it was a relief to know he was capable after what they'd gone through.

Addie hauled him inside, and Belay, who'd been staying with Addie because Evan had flown for this trip, pressed against his thigh, demanding attention. After she was satisfied with his greeting, she sniffed her dog bed in the corner of the living room and settled in like she could finally relax because all of her people were under one roof.

*Me too, Bel. Me too.*

"I can't believe you're here! How did you get back early? What happened? Is everything okay?"

Her onslaught of questions made him grin. "I caught an earlier flight because I couldn't go another night without seeing you. Other than that, everything is fine. Is Sawyer asleep?"

"Yep."

He'd assumed as much. "I'm bummed that I missed him."

"Every time I think I couldn't love you more, I see you loving Sawyer and I just…" Her shoulders inched up, her voice watery. "I fall a little further." Her eyes widened. "Are you hungry? Do you want anything to eat or drink? I'm sure you're exhausted."

Evan caught her hand as she moved toward the fridge in the small kitchen and tugged her back to him. "I don't need anything. Just you." He tucked her against his chest, his arms snug around her and hers around him. "What if you just kept falling? Would that be so bad?"

"Do I have any other choice?" From her spot nestled under his chin, her words held a smile.

"So then if we got married, it would only make sense."

Her fingers, which had been idly tracing across his back, froze.

Evan swallowed—not that it helped create any saliva—and continued. "And then instead of coming here to visit you, I'd be coming home right now. To you and Sawyer."

Addie stiffened inside his hold, and his lungs flat quit. A good five years passed. And then she was shoving away from him, searching his face. "Are you for real? Are you asking me to marry you or just floating the idea around?"

"Asking." Because he'd figured out how to stay. Because when he struggled in that area, he could talk to Addie about it and she'd help him. Because God would help him to choose her and Sawyer over and over again—not like that was a chore. And because his dad's actions no longer controlled him. No longer held him captive. Evan was free.

Her cheeks creased. "Yes." She threw herself at him—again. She and Sawyer both had that habit now, and Evan had happily adjusted to it. Even if they did knock him off-balance from time to time. He was just glad they believed him capable of catching them. Because he finally believed the same about himself.

He freed an arm in order to slip the ring box from his back pocket.

When she released him, he held it out, then thought to open it.

Addie covered her cheeks with her hands. "Oh my, oh my, oh my. I thought you'd just stumbled into saying something about getting married. I didn't know you'd planned it." She sucked in a breath, her hands doing that girly flapping thing that Evan still didn't—and probably never would—understand.

"I planned on you, honey. I'm always going to plan on you."

Moisture shimmered in her mesmerizing eyes. "What did I ever do without you, Evan Hawke?"

"The better question is how did I ever survive without you?" And the answer? He had been doing simply that before Addie—surviving but not truly *living*.

And now? He had a whole lot of life in front of him.

In front of *them*.

\* \* \* \* \*

*Don't miss these other books in Jill Lynn's*
*Colorado Grooms miniseries:*

The Rancher's Surprise Daughter
The Rancher's Unexpected Baby
The Bull Rider's Secret

Dear Reader,

Thank you for continuing to visit Westbend, Colorado, with me. Originally, this series was three books that centered around Wilder Ranch. But once Evan Hawke became part of his brother's story in book three, I wanted him to have his own. I loved who he'd become after the trauma he'd been through. Of course, each of us has our issues, just like Addie and Evan, and we're all works in progress. I'm so thankful we have a God whose love isn't dependent on our actions.

A book is a joint effort. These pages wouldn't exist without God, friends who help brainstorm, my family, my editor and you. Thank you for reading and supporting Christian fiction. As always, any mistakes in research are all mine.

I'd love to connect with you. I'm online at https://www.facebook.com/JillLynnAuthor/ and https://www.instagram.com/jilllynnauthor/, and my current giveaway and newsletter sign-up can be found at http://jill-lynn.com/news/.

*Jill*